The Big Fifty

1/16/2002

Dr. Joe,

I just wanted to
thank you for all you done done
for my family over the years.
Hope you enjoy the 'story'...

Jyb. Warburton

The Big Fifty

Jay S. Warburton

Writers Club Press
San Jose New York Lincoln Shanghai

The Big Fifty

Writers Club Press
an imprint of iUniverse.com, Inc.

For information address:
iUniverse.com, Inc.
5220 S 16th, Ste. 200
Lincoln, NE 68512
www.iuniverse.com

ISBN: 0-595-15648-7

Printed in the United States of America

This novel is dedicated to my wonderful wife, Nancy, and our daughter, Valerie. As anyone who has ever undertaken serious writing of any form knows, it can often be a self-centered and isolated project. Nancy and Val's patience and understanding helped make this book possible and without their support I doubt that I would have finished it.

There are numerous people whom I could thank for their input and constant support while I was penning this story, but my wife, Nancy, deserves the most credit. She helped me numerous times as I tried to break through a number of roadblocks that stopped my progress.

Second in line has to be my copy editor, Stephanie G'Schwind. I'm certain she had her doubts as to what she ventured into when she started editing this manuscript. I have to say that without her help I would have been completely lost. She was super to work with and she deserves a special thanks.

Author's Note

The Big Fifty is a work of fiction. All of the characters and situations created in this novel are fictional and any similarity to real people or events is coincidental.

Chapter *One*

The crowd noise was so loud it was impossible to hear the announcer, much less the loud, dull thud I was repeating as fast as my arm could come down on the bass drum. Mr. Calhoun, our band director, completely gave up trying to organize our twenty-member pep band into playing anything.

The thousand or so parents, students, and other fans in the bleachers were on their feet jumping up and down, shouting at the top of their lungs, and across the rink the Poudre High School crowd was doing the same thing.

Bill Jackson, the left wing for the Poudre Panthers, was skating all alone down the center of the ice directly toward Gill Howard, our goalie. The closest defender was Walt Greecy, a good twenty feet back but bent over in a power stride and at a 45-degree angle to Bill. Bill was tearing down the ice, brooming the puck back and forth, eyes glued directly on Gill.

Gill was hunched down, covering as much of the net as he could, moving out to meet Bill's challenge. Fifteen feet out, Bill lifted his stick and slapped the puck as hard as he could directly at Gill. At that same instant Walt left his skates and threw his body like a human arrow directly between the puck's path and the net Gill was trying to protect.

Walt couldn't have timed his leap better, sliding along the ice to intercept the streaming puck five feet in front of Gill and the overtime sudden-death goal that would have ended our hockey season and given us a second-place city championship.

The puck careened off of Walt's mid-section, bouncing back and over Bill's stick, preventing him from taking a second shot from the rebounding puck.

Directly behind Bill was Rick Maloney, our right wing. Rick slid his stick around the backside of the puck and leaned into the ice. Skates slicing the ice, he turned into a swift arch back up the ice into Panther territory.

Bob Price, the Panthers' center, was the only defender between Rick and our left wing, "Slick" Willie Broomfield. Slick raced to position on the left side of the Panthers' goalie. Rick circled out to the right and faked a slap shot, making Bob commit and crouch to defend against the shot. When Bob committed, Rick passed the puck right behind Bob directly into the face of Slick's stick. Immediately Slick pulled the trigger and fired the puck toward the Panthers' net.

The Panthers' goalie couldn't make the readjustment from his defensive stance against Rick's fake shot, and Slick slapped the puck as hard as he could right into the unprotected left corner of the Panthers' goal.

Instantly pandemonium broke out on our side of the rink. I was pounding the pud out of my bass drum and screaming at the top of my lungs. Down on the ice the entire Pikes Peak High School Indians team was piling on top of Slick. We were the 1962 Colorado Springs city high school hockey champions.

All I can remember of the next fifteen or so seconds was looking off to the right of the celebrating pile of Pikes Peak players over at the Panthers' bench. In unison all of the Panther players stood and held their hands and arms extended high into the air with their middle fingers sticking straight up, flipping them directly across the rink toward our side of the arena. The noise inside that building was so loud I couldn't hear what they were shouting to back up their single-finger salute, but I could read their lips; if they had been girls, I would loved to have taken them up on their offer.

I sure wasn't the only one in the stands who saw the Panthers' gesture—the finger that was fired and heard around the entire Brookshire International Ice Palace. In fact, I would have to say a good 90 percent of the Indian student body there saw the salute.

The following thirty minutes would change my entire life, along with those of eleven of my high school buddies.

There was a fraction of a second of silence, letting the reality of the Panthers' gesture register in our minds. Then all hell broke loose.

The only protective glass curved around each end of the arena. The center section on both sides of the rink was separated from the crowd by a four-foot-high wooden retainer wall allowing easy access to the ice simply by hopping over it.

Mr. Calhoun instantly stood and turned toward us from below. His eyes were icy and piercing as he shouted, "Sit down and don't move! Now!"

Howie Jones stepped down one bleacher past Mr. Calhoun as Mr. Calhoun's hand shot out and grabbed Howie. Howie's trumpet popped out of his left hand as Mr. Calhoun sat him down hard. The rest of us stayed put.

Because we were all sitting in a block of the bleachers behind the crowd and at the top of the stadium, we were easily corralled by Mr. Calhoun.

It looked like a molten flow of people moving in one mass toward the guardrail and onto the ice. When the initial wave of Indian students hopped over the wooden barrier, they were so intent on reaching the other side of the rink they forgot about the ice directly underfoot. Bodies were upending and flying in all sorts of contorted ways just prior to slapping down hard on the rock-hard ice. Those who followed learned from their comrades and immediately started to make their advance in a stiff, zombie-like strut. Some still couldn't stay upright on the slippery ice and took other victims down with them as they grasped for anything and anybody to support themselves. It looked like an advancing army being slaughtered, only there weren't any bullets being fired. Some students hit the ice and didn't move again, and their comrades didn't seem to care as they pushed on en masse toward the enemy.

When the Panthers' spectators saw the Indian uprising coming across the ice, their masses advanced down the bleachers. There was the same reaction by the initial wave of Panthers hitting the ice with flattened bodies being stepped over and on, moving forward to engage the enemy.

Just before the two armies made their initial clash, Sheriff "Daddy" Bruce's voice boomed at ear-cracking decibels over the intercom speakers overhead. The loud burst of his voice brought both student bodies to a slow, sliding halt of sorts; it was quite apparent that most everybody didn't know how to stop their forward motion on the ice any better than they knew how to get started. Again, both sides suffered unbelievable casualties of falling bodies being cut down in battle by invisible bullets.

Actually the *first* words of wisdom over the speakers was from a benign voice of an uncaring announcer asking the rampant mobs of students to "Please leave the—" just before Sheriff Bruce's voice shattered our eardrums with "HEY! EVERYBODY STOP RIGHT WHERE YOU ARE!"

I don't think Sheriff Bruce realized how hard that was for a couple hundred kids on ice. It was like watching all of them playing a slow-motion yard game of Mother May I?

By this time in the early moments in the Battle of the Brookshire Ice Palace, both coaches from each side had entered the arena, trying to quell the advancing battalions. The only problem with this was that they reacted only to the mob scene taking place before them but neglected to tell their respective players to head back to the locker rooms. When they saw their generals heading out onto the field of battle, the hockey players just followed like a well-trained squadron.

Just when the battle looked like it was going to be stopped before it started, Sheriff Bruce dropped his microphone and threw open the west-end gate and strutted authoritatively out onto the ice. As soon as the smooth soles of his spit-polished patrolman's boots hit the slick ice, he began the most spectacular aerial demonstration of versatility a suspended human body has ever done. I believe he achieved six or seven feet of horizontal elevation. He looked, at one instant, as though he were trying to make an aerial snow angel and at the very next, trying to perfect his backstroke. His hat, of course, along with his glasses, left his head the instant he became airborne.

When his attempt at trying to right himself via the backstroke failed, he actually tried to land upright by making a very awkward attempt at doing a backward somersault in mid-air. With arms and legs flailing away at all angles, I'll have to admit it wasn't a pretty sight, but he did manage to make the 180 just before hitting the ice flat out and face down with a splat that shook fear into anyone who cared.

If there was anyone who cared, their thoughts of "poor ol' Daddy" completely disappeared when the force from his impact on the ice popped open the holster strap holding his .38 pistol. The gun shot out of the holster and went skittering across the ice in a perfectly straight line down the center of the length of the rink. It sailed down precisely between the two groups of students, coaches, and players, drawing an invisible "line in the ice" between the two armies.

All the eyes in the arena were drawn away from the flattened, unmoving sheriff and were glued to the spinning pistol, which finally made it completely across the entire length of the rink and slowly eased up to the side boards with a quiet "clunk."

To this day I truly believe the ensuing battle would have ended right there if the Panthers' Coach Sloakum would have just moved a bit more to his right as he pushed his way toward the front of the mob of Panther students. Of course, it wasn't Sloakum's fault that he moved right in front of one of his players, who was trying to catch up to his coach. I still don't know the kid's name, but when he upended Coach Sloakum, sending him feet-first across the "line in the ice" and directly into the advancing Indians' Coach Svensen, who then dipped and landed right on top of Coach Sloakum. Any chance for a peaceful end to this event was squashed right then and there.

Even though both coaches were just trying to get up, it sure looked like they were having a horizontal fistfight to anyone watching, and, at that moment everybody in the entire arena was looking right down at them.

Chapter *Two*

By the time the two coaches untangled themselves and reached their feet, the two mobs of students had crossed the line. Shouting was the first weapon used, followed by some rampant shoving until the first fist flew.

From my viewpoint high in the stands, it was impossible to see who hit whom, but it resulted in an all-out brawl. Young bodies were falling all over the ice, and the shouting had turned to screaming and panic. Even a few girls were swinging and kicking their arms and legs in all directions.

The celebrating pile of Indian players was overrun by the two battling mobs of students when someone hollered, "Sloakum's beating up Coach Svensen!"

The pile quickly unfolded. Jim Henry was the first Indian player on his feet. When he saw the Panther players skating onto the ice and into the fight, he shouted, "They're beating up Coach!"

In a wedge of maroon and gold jerseys, they skated right into the mass of fighting and falling bodies of battle. "Get 'em!" was screamed out by one of the Panther players, and the two teams clashed in the middle of the melee.

About this time something struck me on the side of my face and made me jump. Instantly I looked toward the direction I thought it was coming from. "Jensen!" Mr. Calhoun was looking directly at me. He had thrown a score book at me to get my attention.

"Get your drum, and all of the rest of you follow me right now!" He started to move down the bleachers toward the entrance to the ice arena. All of us followed Mr. Calhoun like a covey of quail behind the mother as we watched the fight below us out on the ice.

"Don't stop! Just follow me out the door and go directly to the bus!"

As we moved single file around the outside curve of the rink to the main entrance, the mass of students on the ice shifted toward the entrance right toward us. Indian players were dragging Panther players by their arms, legs, and anything else they could get hold of, and some of the students were helping them.

Even though the coaches were up and doing their best to squelch the fighting, their attempts to regain order were lost in the chaos of the battle. Other security guards had arrived, but their efforts were futile in the mass confusion.

At the other end of the rink, Sheriff Bruce was being helped off the ice and didn't have the slightest idea of what was going on around him.

The Brookshire International Ice Palace was only one of many complexes that surrounded a twenty-acre oval-shaped lake. The Palace was located on the southwest corner of the lake; just to the north was the first of two golf courses. To the north of the courses, separated by a parking lot, was the Penrose Rodeo Stadium. And at the north end of the stadium, there was a small bridge leading out from the sidewalk to a small island in the middle of the lake. On the east shoreline was the world-famous Brookshire Hotel. All of this encompassed the most beautiful resort in the Rocky Mountain West. This hotel resort was built in the late 1800s by an English gentleman who had struck it rich in the gold field of Cripple Creek some sixty miles to the west. Spencer Penrose chose this sight for his luxurious hotel because of its beautiful location on the foothills of majestic Cheyenne Mountain, which towered twelve thousand feet into the brilliant blue skies. The Brookshire

Hotel was the hub of the West's most elite and wealthy community. Situated on a sloping plateau, the community of million-dollar houses and estates overlooked the city of Colorado Springs, Colorado, to the north. Only because of the Brookshire and its Ice Palace were the high schools in the region able to have hockey teams.

The entire lake had a walkway around it that was landscaped to perfection with towering blue spruce evergreens spaced perfectly so the main hotel was framed between the trees. The walkway was illuminated by the soft light that radiated from Old English-styled bulb lampposts. A quiet, romantic air engulfed the grounds and lake, making it a distinctive destination resort for the rich and famous from all over the world.

Weaving our way around the east end of the rink, Mr. Calhoun turned and waved us to follow him forward. "Hurry!" he shouted as he turned into the corridor leading us out the front entrance to the Palace.

Just as all of us were hurrying along behind Mr. Calhoun, the gates to this end of the rink were forced open by the mass of screaming and fighting students. Mr. Calhoun was the first one out the swinging glass doors and was standing outside facing us and directing everyone to the right like a traffic cop, pointing toward the parking lot and the school bus. We filed past him as all of us were turning back to look at the mob coming right on our heels.

Some of the Indian players and students had hoisted a few of the Panther players in the air high over their heads. The chant "Throw them in the lake!" resounded above all the other racket.

We moved single file right past Mr. Calhoun and out of the way of the onslaught of the mob. But Mr. Calhoun didn't move out of the way of the approaching mob: he took a gallant stand between them and the lake.

"STOP!" he screamed at the top of his lungs, both hands held straight up in the air. "OH SHIT!" was the last we heard from him—and the last we saw of him—just before he was pushed backward into the ice-cold lake. At least he had the honor of being the first one in the lake, but only for a short instant.

The entire pep band was now huddled together on the sidelines watching the forced march of students and players into the lake. Mr. Calhoun was followed by a Panther player lofted into the air, screaming, "Nooo!" He hit the water with a huge splash, and the screaming chants of the students changed again to shouts of triumph as more Panther players were thrown into the water. Then it turned into a complete free-for-all. The slow forward motion of the crowd turned into a panic of kids in the front trying to turn back into the crowd away from the water's edge. Behind them was a force of humanity trying to get closer to the action on the lakeshore. Just like lemmings, wave after wave of students were forced into the icy water of the lake, and shouts of triumph quickly turned to screams of shock as warm bodies hit the cold water. Somewhere in that mass of floundering humanity was Mr. Calhoun. I remember seeing him only once as he was standing in waist-deep water trying, almost successfully, to get back up on the shore only to be knocked back into the lake.

Before the dry side of the mob finally reversed its flow into the lake, nine Panther players and three of the Indian players were in the lake along with thirty or forty students, plus Mr. Calhoun.

By this time the fear of the fighting mob was subsiding and all of us in the band were laughing hysterically, as were a good share of the crowd of students. While we were enjoying the rowdy, wet scene before us, none of us noticed that a group of Panther students had surrounded us.

Chapter *Three*

Before I could do anything about it, one of the Panther boys grabbed the drumstick out of my hand and started beating me over the head with it. I was holding the bass drum in front of me with one hand on each side gripping the rims, the drum vertical to the ground. The kid hitting me was close to six feet tall and built like a fullback. His first blows to my head knocked my glasses off, and after they hit the ground beside me, I heard the crackling sound of lenses breaking under the foot of another Panther boy standing behind me.

"Leave him alone!" Jennifer Lucas shouted, and I saw her move in behind me, shoving hard the kid who had stepped on my glasses. Jennifer was a junior, played the flute, and was my girlfriend. She pushed the kid hard enough to knock him a little off balance, and as he staggered backward she swung her flute around her backside, up over her head, and brought it down hard right on top of the boy's head. He dropped like a brick—the blow from Jennifer's flute cold-cocked him.

I was bending over and trying to duck my head as best I could while holding the drum, but I couldn't escape the blows to my head. I grasped the edges of the big drum as tight as I could and swayed to my left to get as much leverage as I could muster. I moved my left foot behind me to brace myself and swung the drum back around to my right with all the force I had. The right rim of the drum and its full size hit the mid-section of the big kid who was hitting me with the stick. I heard something make a loud popping sound like the wooden rim of the drum snapping. The kid bent over, dropped the stick, and fell to the ground, hitting his butt real hard. On his way down he grabbed his left side and let out a loud groan. When he hit the ground the impact knocked the wind out of him, and he keeled over holding his left rib cage.

Before I knew what else was happening around me, Jennifer grabbed the outer rim of my drum and yanked forward. "Run for the bus!" she shouted, pulling me toward the big orange blur in the distance. Without my glasses I couldn't see anything in focus and followed along behind her as she pulled and directed me through parked cars to the bus.

All the other band members had run for the bus as soon as they saw the big kid grab my stick and start beating me with it.

"Thanks for all of your help, you big bunch of chicken shits," I said, scanning the whole group, who were stacked up behind one another and glaring out the windows of the bus to watch the chaos still going on in front of the Palace. "Yeah. You guys are really something," Jennifer said, backing me up with her own choice set of words.

I checked the side of the drum to see where it was cracked, but there were only a few scratches along the outside rim, and the skin had a hole in the center. I turned to Jennifer. "Must have broken that kid's ribs." She smiled. Other than a slight dent, her flute was just fine.

I rolled the big drum down the center aisle between the rows of seats to the back of the bus. Jennifer and I turned to look out the windows of the bus doors.

By this time sirens could be heard and flashing lights atop half a dozen police cars were flashing in the parking lot in front of us. A dozen or so cops were now mingling through the huge crowd of students. There were still a couple dozen kids in the lake trying to work their way back to the shore. Two cops were giving as many of them a helping hand as they could. Every kid the cops could get hold of was ushered back into the lobby of the Palace.

"Hey, check out Elmer Fudd trying to help Calhoun out of the lake!" someone shouted. Elmer Fudd was the nickname we had for our principal, Mr. Fluorite, because he looked exactly like the cartoon character. He extended a hand to Mr. Calhoun, pulling him up onto dry land. He even took off his suit coat and offered it to our band leader. Mr. Calhoun pushed the offer away and said something to Mr. Fluorite, then turned, heading for the bus. We could tell by his determined gait that his arrival wasn't going to be pleasant. All of us scrambled to our seats and sat quietly.

Jennifer leaned over toward me and kissed my forehead. "Are you hurt?" I shook my head in a negative reply and grasped her hand in mine.

Jennifer was gorgeous. Five feet, six inches tall with an hour-glass figure, she was my pride and joy. We had been going steady for over a year. I met her in band when she came to Pikes Peak High as a transfer student from Scottsbluff, Nebraska. After the first set of tryouts for the flute section, Mr. Calhoun placed her in the first chair, and she'd stayed there ever since. Her shoulder-length auburn hair always had a slight inward curl at the base, with an easy sweep backward across her temples. Her bangs were cut about halfway down her forehead and really accented her dark brown eyes. Her face was thin and delicately featured with slight dimples in each cheek when she smiled, and her eyes sparkled almost all the time. She liked to wear knee-high skirts that swayed seductively as she walked. I know I was a bit biased, but Jennifer was one heck of a beautiful girl.

The bus doors flew open. "Where's Ben?!" Mr. Calhoun screamed. Right behind him Mr. Ben, our bus driver, appeared out of nowhere. Mr. Calhoun stepped aside to let him through to his driver's seat. He looked down at Mr. Ben and growled, "Get this bus back to the school right now." He grabbed hold of the support pole directly behind Mr. Ben's seat and swung himself around and into his seat right behind Ben.

"You all right, Mr. Calhoun?" Sue Hackley, the only freshman member of the pep band, asked with as much sympathy in her voice as she could muster. He didn't say a word, just looked straight ahead at the back of Mr. Ben's head.

Jennifer and I were in the seats right across from Mr. Calhoun. I was in the aisle seat three feet from him and could smell the musty odor from the lake that completely soaked his clothes. Looking out of the corner of my eye down toward his feet, I could see a little puddle of water slowly growing around both of his wing-tipped shoes. I had a sly smile on my face when Jennifer jabbed me lightly in the ribs with her elbow; she was right—it was in my best interest to just sit there expressionless.

Jennifer and I turned toward the window as the bus pulled away. There were still a few kids scuffling in front of the Palace, but for the most part the crowd had dispersed. A few isolated groups of three or four kids stood around in disbelief of what had just taken place.

As we left the parking lot and headed down Mountain View Avenue toward our high school, we spotted some boys darting in and around parked cars. Some of them who cleared the lot were running as fast as they could. Mr. Calhoun remained motionless and never said a word all the way back to the school.

Chapter *Four*

My name is Ralph Jensen, but all of my high school buddies called me Rock, which was the nickname given to a bass drummer in a band. My parents moved down to Colorado from Devil's Lake, North Dakota, in 1955, when I was a fifth-grader. Dad was a warehouse manager for the Nash Finch Company in Devil's Lake when he came up with an advertising idea for the tourist industry and decided to strike out on his own. He loved the Rocky Mountain West and chose Colorado Springs to start his entrepreneurial venture because the Springs was the hub of the tourist business in the West. The Springs used to boast that it had more motels than all the states of Minnesota, North Dakota, and South Dakota combined. It was also one of the main destination points for vacationers from all over the United States and abroad. The city is located at the very foot of the world-famous Pike's Peak, which rises above the city to a height of over twelve thousand feet above sea level. Obviously, you can see where my high school got its name. Famous gold-mining camps such as Cripple Creek and Victor were sixty miles to the west, destination points for pioneers heading out from St. Louis to Colorado to strike it rich. Their covered wagons were painted with the slogan "Pike's Peak or Bust!"—and most of them returned to the Midwest busted. The exquisite beauty of the area and the rich gold ore found by a few such as Spencer Penrose, however, enticed them to stay and build a town. Thus, the Brookshire Hotel and Resort rose at the foot of Cheyenne Mountain, one of the front-range sister mountains to the Peak. Financed by Penrose and other investors from his homeland of England, the Brookshire was built and became a world-renowned resort in the rough-and-tumble great American West.

Penrose's dream resort had to have everything a "greenhorn" would want: world-class accommodations, fine food and service, and a multitude of recreational opportunities. He wanted the main complex of buildings to encircle a private lake, so he built one. Because rodeo was a major Western sport and attraction, he built the Penrose Stadium directly across the lake from the main hotel. Professional ice-skating was an elitist sport at the time and one that he loved, so Penrose had the Ice Palace constructed. He knew the rich and famous love golf and tennis, so two fabulous golf courses and enclosed clay tennis courts were added. Plus, because of his love for wild animals, the highest zoo in the world was constructed a few miles up the mountain and called the Cheyenne Mountain Zoo. So his visitors could reach the zoo directly from the hotel grounds, Penrose had a miniature train system built to take them up the mountain to the zoo, and along the route they were treated to the views of the mountain vistas and a tour of the gorgeously landscaped golf courses. He was also concerned about the possible extinction of one of the West's most romantic creatures and had a natural area along the train route enclosed to hold a small herd of buffalo.

The main hotel was built to the exact specifications of the most luxurious English architectural designs of that era. Every visitor was greeted by beautifully carved granite water fountains surrounded by rich green, manicured lawns landscaped with gorgeous beds of flowers that gave the crisp mountain air a fresh, sweet fragrance. Indoors, from the rich marble floors to the satin-covered walls and huge cut-glass chandeliers hanging from every great room in the building, absolutely no expense was spared. Every guest was to be treated as royalty, with every whim catered to by red-coated employees.

The hotel offered the finest food, prepared by world-renowned chefs in a number of different restaurants, each of which was set in an elegant atmosphere. Indoor swimming pools, a drug store and soda fountain, English pubs, a movie theater, and nearly every other amenity one could want or imagine was enclosed under the eight-story spheroid Colorado hotel.

On the backside of the hotel, a huge marble plaza led the guests to the edge of the lake. Here is where all of the fancy balls were held throughout the cool summer evenings. Grand pianos and the finest pianists played romantic music for the folks dressed in tuxedos and elegant gowns. Directly north of the plaza, on the lake's edge, an outdoor heated pool refreshed the guests during the heat of the day. The view to the west looked out over the blue waters of the lake to the Ice Palace and over the roof of the rodeo stadium up to the majestic Cheyenne Mountain and Pikes Peak to its north.

Education of the area children was a main concern and the finest of school systems in the West was built. Nothing was neglected when it came to education, and the Brookshire school system grew to be known as one of the finest in the state—and the wealthiest. My folks wanted the best for me and my sister and our three brothers.

The residential area of the Brookshire community was actually built on a huge, high-rolling foothill at the base of Cheyenne Mountain, which gradually sloped downhill to a lowland area to the north. Upper-middle-class families built homes down in this region, which was still in the Brookshire school district. My folks purchased a home in the Skyway Park housing development on Salano Drive.

There were two basic classes of kids at Pikes Peak High School: the rich kids, who lived up on "the hill," and the rest of us. The sports were also separated according to the student's family wealth. In order to make the team on the more respected and accepted sports like football, basketball, swimming, and baseball, a kid had to be an exceptional athlete unless he lived on "the hill." Track and hockey were open to the rest of us. With the exception of Jack Peterson and Bobby Hunt, both juniors, the rest of the hockey team was made up of boys from the lowlands.

As for me, I was damned near blind without my glasses, and at five feet seven and 130 pounds, I wasn't cut out for many sports. But I loved music.

Chapter *Five*

When the bus pulled up to the front of the school, all of us filed out of the bus as quietly and quickly as possible. Not even a whisper could be heard.

Mr. Calhoun just sat in his seat looking straight ahead. Even Mr. Ben didn't say a word, only nodding his head to each student as we turned to depart out the bus doors.

Jennifer and I were the first ones out, and we led the rest of the band members up the winding sidewalk to the outside doors of the band room. Whispers were bantered back and forth throughout the group.

"Isn't he gonna come and unlock the door?" Jennifer softly asked me.

I turned and saw Mr. Calhoun step down off the bus with an over-the-shoulder wave good-bye to Mr. Ben; I don't know if he said anything at all to the bus driver. I then saw the bus doors swing shut, heard the bus engine rev up, and watched the big orange vehicle move out of the lot.

"He's coming," I said to Jennifer. "Just be quiet and let him through."

Nobody said a thing as Mr. Calhoun weaved his way through the crowd of kids. He had to hold his right pants-pocket down with his left hand to keep his wet pocket from clinging to his other hand when he reached in to retrieve the keys to the band-room door.

Still not muttering a word, Mr. Calhoun unlocked the door and swung it open. Just before he stepped inside ahead of us, he said with a firm, low voice, "Put your instruments away and go straight home."

Sue Hackley was the only one who said anything to him.

"Are you OK, Mr. Calhoun?"

Mr. Calhoun was a dark-complexioned man of middle age and stood a sturdy six feet. Because of his dark complexion, his pitch-black eyes were highlighted, making them seem piercing when he looked at you. The look he gave Sue froze her in her tracks, and her shoulders drooped down noticeably. He didn't say a word, and Sue turned slowly away from him, walking a couple of short steps before scurrying over to the cabinet across the room where she stored her clarinet. She opened the cabinet door and quickly put the clarinet on the top shelf, turned around, and walked briskly out of the room.

Jennifer helped me lift my drum onto its metal stand at the back of the risers in the percussion section on the back row. Looking at me over the top of the drum and nodding her head toward the door, she whispered, "I'm taking my flute home. Let's get out of here."

Most of the other kids were already gone as we stepped down the risers to the door. Mr. Calhoun had closed the door to his little cubicle office next to the exit. Both of us casually glanced through the tiny square window as we walked right past. He was sitting in his low-backed hardwood swivel chair with both elbows on his desk cradling his head in his hands.

About halfway down the sidewalk to the parking lot, a half-dozen other band members were huddled in a loose circle.

All of them turned and slowly walked toward Jennifer and me as we moved down the walk toward them. Jim Blair, a tall, skinny six-foot senior with thick brown hair combed back in a ducktail, was the first to speak. With both hands in the pockets of his blue jeans, he snapped his head back, motioning toward the band room. "Boy howdy, was he pissed." The others were shaking their heads in various motions indicating agreement with Jim's assessment.

Mary Schlonicker, Jim's girlfriend, looked right at me. "What do you think is gonna happen?"

Mary was a senior also and one of the prettiest girls in our school. She and Jim had been going steady since junior high. They were seldom seen without each other, and the rumor around school was they were going to be get married shortly after graduation. I'll have to admit, they looked like the perfect couple and never had a bad argument. Mary's petite frame complemented Jim's thin height well, and she had a knock-out figure with blonde hair that she almost always kept pulled back in a tight ponytail. Her golden hair and thin matching eyebrows accented her beautiful facial features: high cheekbones, dark blue eyes, and smooth golden skin. Most of the boys were jealous of Jim, and when Mary even glanced their way their hearts would melt with desire.

"Hell, Mary, I don't know, but it's not gonna be pretty around this place come Monday morning," I said.

"But we didn't do anything!" Billy Ewing was a heavy-set sophomore trumpet player and always talked with a whining ring to his voice. When he spoke this time, his voice was a good two octaves higher than normal and grated on my brain.

"Just shut up, shit-head," someone said, and Billy kind of slinked off to one side.

"Come on, guys. Leave Billy alone," Jennifer said with a firm voice.

Before everybody started arguing, I turned and pointed back toward the band room where Mr. Calhoun sat behind a locked door with his back to us.

"Let's get out of here and meet at the Pard. Everybody'll be there," I said, grabbing Jennifer by her hand. I walked in front, towing her behind me in the direction of the student parking lot. The rest of the kids followed.

"What do you think *will* happen next Monday, honey?" Jennifer asked with a firm grip on my hand and a little skip to catch up with me. "We're in deep shit, aren't we?"

I looked down into her emerald eyes and gave her a quick kiss, then turned and picked up our step to the car. "No shit," I said. "You'll have to drive because I can't see a damn thing."

Just as Jennifer drove us out of the lot, the team school bus was turning into the back of the school behind the gymnasium. All of the lights were out. We'd hear about everything in a little while when everyone gathered at the Pard.

Chapter *Six*

"Pard" was short for the Howdy Pard, a drive-in hamburger stand on north Eighth Street. It was about five miles from school and a common hangout for all of the kids from Pikes Peak High. Located on the east side of a four-lane road, it was easy to spot as you crested the Eighth Street hill, leading down from the Brookshire lowlands residential area. The stand's neon sign was one of the brightest and most unique along that section of the road—a miniature replica of the much bigger and famous cowboy neon sign on the downtown strip of Las Vegas. Although the lights didn't move in animation like the Vegas version, the smaller sign's bright orange, red, and green tubular gas lights did flash on and off at regular intervals every few seconds.

The Pard didn't have an indoor eating area, just a metal-railed drive-up lane with six speakers for placing orders. Each speaker was placed a little over a car's length apart all the way up to the pick-up window. Mr. Harding and his wife, Lydia, owned and ran the place. Specializing in shakes, malts, hamburgers, cheeseburgers, curly-Q fries, and onion rings, the Pard was the number-one destination for Pikes Peak High students. Mr. Harding made the best shakes and flavored Cokes— cherry, vanilla, and chocolate—plus Green and Red Rivers. When you ordered a burger, fries, and a Coke from the Hardings, you got a hefty order and never went away hungry. The shakes were always thick and filled to the top of the big paper cup; the burger was thick, juicy, and loaded with all the goodies between freshly baked buns and wrapped in a couple of sheets of crisp tissue paper. The fries or rings filled a thin cardboard boat to overflowing with two Dixie cups of catsup on the side, plus plenty of small packets of salt.

Almost any night of the week, the huge gravel parking lot surrounding the Pard was completely packed with Indian students' cars. Four bright floodlights were mounted on tall telephone poles in each corner of the lot, completely lighting up the area. When the weather was cold, rainy, or snowing, the cars would be parked side by side, headlights to taillights, with a constant buzz of teenage conversation crossing between rolled-down car windows. On warm summer nights the Pard lot was filled with kids roaming from one huddle to the next. Because the Hardings didn't think teenagers should be out too late on school nights, they closed the place down promptly at 10:30 and announced over their outdoor PA speakers, "Thanks for your business. It's time to call it a night and head for home," and they turned out the lights except for those inside the tiny rectangular building. On Friday, Saturday, and summer evenings, they stayed open until midnight.

I was sitting with my back against the passenger door and my left leg bent and resting on the bench seat between Jennifer and me when we turned into the Pard's drive-up lane. "What do you want?" she asked looking straight ahead and easing up to the third speaker behind the two cars ahead of us.

"Give me a large cherry Coke, and let's split a large fry."

Mrs. Harding's voice crackled loudly from the metal megaphone speaker, "Can I help you?"

Jennifer placed my order, plus a medium vanilla Coke for herself.

The November air was chilly but calm, so I had my window rolled down.

"Hey, Jensen! Damn that was somethin' else after the game. Cool, man." Dave Harrison tapped me on the shoulder and bent down peering past me over to Jennifer. "How ya doin', gorgeous? You chauffeuring the Rock around these days? I didn't think he'd let anybody drive old Ironsides besides himself." Just then Dave lifted his hand from the window ledge of the door and pointed at my face. "I knew something was different. Where the heck are your glasses?"

Before I could say anything, Jennifer bent over toward me and looked up at Dave. "A couple of bozos jumped us after the game and knocked 'em off his face and stepped on them."

The second car ahead of us got their order and pulled out into the lot. They were a couple of older folks and turned back toward the entrance and left. Harry Bonner and his girl, Carol Harbor, were wrapped arm in arm, necking in the car directly ahead of us and didn't notice the car in front of them pulling out. Jennifer tapped the horn, and they slowly released each other and looked back at us. Harry gave us a backhanded wave and, with a smile on his face, turned and put his '56 Chevy in gear, pulling forward to the window.

Old Ironsides was a brown four-door '54 straight-eight Pontiac with an automatic transmission. Jennifer had it in park and forgot to shift it down, racing the engine when she stepped on the accelerator. "Got to slip her into 'D' for drive," I said with a cocky smile. She dropped the gearshift handle and moved ahead slowly, hitting me hard on my left shoulder. "I know. I know." She pulled up behind Harry and Carol, who were already being handed their order from Mrs. Harding. When they pulled out Jennifer eased up to the window, and while we were moving forward Dave opened the back door and hopped in.

"Here you go, kids," Mrs. Harding said, leaning out the drive-up window. "That'll be $1.54."

I counted out the change into Jennifer's hand, and she handed it to Mrs. Harding. As she turned toward the cash register, Mrs. Harding did a double-take and peered back into our window, looking past Jennifer to me. "What happened to your glasses, Ralph?"

"A Poudre kid knocked them off and broke them at the rink after the game," I said.

Just then Mr. Harding came over and leaned over his wife's shoulder. "We heard about the big fight up there. Sounded pretty bad. Something like a dozen or so kids were actually arrested. They didn't give out any of the names, though. Sure hope none of you kids got hurt. We listened on the radio, and it sounded terrible. At least you guys won the game," he said, shaking his head slightly. "We'll be closing in about fifteen minutes. Glad you and Jenny didn't get hurt. Thanks again for your order."

Jennifer pulled away and moved across the lot to park in a slot between Dave and Carol and a vacant black '58 Ford Fairlane. The air in the lot held the heavy odor of gas fumes from all the idling cars. The blue-gray haze of exhaust fumes hung in the air, producing a foggy look in the floodlights.

"Gawd damn! Was that cool or what after the game? We kicked their ass in the game and after it. Cool, man!" Jerry Altringer slammed the door behind Jennifer as he jumped into the backseat next to Dave. "Did you check out Calhoun? He looked like a drowned rat! What did he say to you guys on the bus?"

"Yeah, man, did he ream you out?" Dave asked with a glint in his eyes.

"He didn't say a thing," I said. "Not a thing. But, man, was he boiling. All of us just dropped our stuff off and got out of there as fast as we could. Even when little Miss Brown-Noser Hackley asked him how he was, he just stared at her and never said a word. He won't be quiet next Monday, though. In fact, I betcha Fudd will call a general assembly and rip our butts. It won't be pretty, but they'll get over it. No sweat."

Just before the Hardings turned off the lot lights, kids were moving toward their cars, some of them already pulling out.

"Looks like Harding's gonna kick us out. Better git." Dave opened his door and stepped out. "Come on, Jerry. Let's leave these love-birds alone."

"Yeah. See ya later." Just before Jerry closed his door, he gave Jennifer a wink and a smile. "Give Jen a juicy kiss for me too, Rock."

"Get outta here, you slob," she said with a chuckle. I sent him away with a "you got it" gesture, forming a circle of approval with my thumb and middle finger.

"We'd better get going too. Besides, I'm starting to get one heck of a headache without my glasses."

"You poor baby," Jennifer said with a soft, seductive tone. We both put our Cokes on the dashboard and moved toward each other into the middle of the seat. Jennifer put her hands on either side of my head, running her the tips of her fingers through my hair and softly across my temples. I put my arms around her and pulled her into me, giving her a tender kiss. Our eyes closed as our lips met, and my headache seemed to fade instantly. The lot went dark.

Pulling away, Jennifer moved her hand to the gearshift and glanced over to Dave's car; the windows were up and covered with steam.

Chapter *Seven*

After picking Jennifer up at her house at seven-thirty Monday morning, we headed up Skyway Park Boulevard toward the high school.

Pikes Peak High was one of the newer schools in the Colorado Springs area. It sat on one of the foothills of the Rocky Mountain Front Range, nestled in among scrub oak trees and a few Ponderosa pines. The entire campus centered around the library, which was a huge A-frame room completely fronted with glass from the roof to the floor. Only the two front doors, made of brown steel, were solid. From almost anywhere in the library you could look out across Colorado Springs and the Great American Plains to the east. With the exception of a few mansions on the hill a quarter of a mile up the mountain behind the school, Pikes Peak High was the highest building in the area. Subconsciously, I think it gave all of us a feeling of superiority over those below us.

The administration offices were directly to the left of the library. Further to the left, along the broad sidewalk canopied by scrub oak trees, were the double doors that led down a short hall, with the art room to the right, and just a little further, the choir room. Centered on the left hallway wall were double doors that were the inside entrance to the band room. At the far end of the hall were a pair of doors that opened to the outside and back of the school.

From the entrance to the band room, choir, and art building, the sidewalk meandered through the scrub oaks about a hundred feet to the cafeteria. Except for the kitchen area, the rest of this building was enclosed in glass. Advanced engineering for the early sixties, the lunchroom was a huge octagonal building with octagonal tables for the students to eat their lunches. On warm fall and spring days, we could eat on redwood tables out on the flagstone patio that encircled the building like a rock moat.

Where the sidewalk leading from the music building met the cafeteria's patio area, the walk split off and headed further down the hill to a large rock-solid-sided building. This was the athletic center, which housed an Olympic-sized swimming pool, basketball courts, and an indoor track and field house. All assemblies were held in this building on the bleachers that surrounded the main basketball court. Directly behind the athletic building and further down the hill was the outdoor track and field, with a separate football field and baseball diamond, all with their own set of bleachers. Below the outfield fence, at the bottom of the hill, was the student parking lot, nearly a quarter of a mile from the library and the remaining wing of the building that housed all the academic classes. A hundred or so feet in front of the library was the visitors' parking lot, and at the north end of the left wing was parking for the faculty.

It was truly a beautiful school in a beautiful setting and held the visual appearance of a miniature university campus.

On any given day the Pikes Peak High student parking lot had cars ranging from old rattle-traps to a brand-new Rolls Royce (one of only three in the entire state of Colorado in 1962). Most of the cars, however, were Fords, Chevys, Nash-Ramblers, with a Dodge here and there and my Pony. They ranged from the early to late fifties, and '56 and '57 Chevys were the prized possessions.

When Jennifer and I pulled old Ironsides into the lot, some of the kids were already working their way up the walk to the school, but most were in small, scattered groups of ten or so, huddled all around the lot.

I pulled into a slot next to Slick Broomfield's '57 Chevy. As we got out of the car, Slick, who was leaning up against the trunk of his car, surrounded by a bunch of other kids, twisted around and pointed up in the direction of the visitors' parking lot. "Check out the bubble-gums parked up there," he said, referring to the black-and-white police cars with the flashing red lights centered on the forward part of the cars' roofs.

"Holy smoke. Looks like we're gonna get lectured to like never before," I said.

"Yeah. And the cops ain't all that's parked up there. Looks like the entire school board is here too," Slick said as he moved away from his car toward the school. He was a big kid, pushing six feet and close to two hundred pounds, but his smooth facial features gave away his youthful look of seventeen. He had both hands in the side pockets of his maroon and white letter jacket, the big 'I' on the right front covered with golden hockey pins. "Jesus, you don't suppose we're gonna get suspended?"

Slick was one of the players involved in throwing a couple of the Panther players into the lake. Jennifer and I walked with him up the walk.

"Hey! Wait up!" Rick Maloney came running up behind us, his letter jacket open and swinging side to side behind him. His flattop haircut made his five-foot-nine frame look even stockier than it was. "What's happenin', man? All kinds of rumors are floating around, and none of them sound good."

As the four of us approached the library, kids were coming back out of the left wing of the school and heading down to the gym. Jim Blair and Mary Schlonicker cut across in front of us. "You're supposed to go check in at your class and head down to the gym for an assembly," Jim said, shrugging his shoulders.

Jennifer let go of my hand as we entered the hallway. "I'll meet you out front after I check in to chemistry," she said.

"OK," I said, cutting across the hall to Mrs. Fowler's English room.

I opened the door, and Mrs. Fowler was sitting behind her old oak desk. She looked up from her attendance book and in a deep, raspy smoker's voice said, "Good morning, Ralph. Please hand in your essay on Daniel Webster and head down to the gym for the general assembly."

I walked up to the front of the room and placed my essay on the stack of other essays building up on the corner of her desk. "Do we come back here after the assembly or go to our next class?" I asked.

Arranging my paper on top of the stack of essays so the pile was perfectly straight and neat, as was everything else on her desk, she said, "I don't know, Ralph. This is a very serious assembly, and it could last for a while. Mr. Fluorite will give the student body instructions when the assembly is over."

"OK, thanks," I said and turned to leave.

Mrs. Fowler was a slight, gray-haired woman in her late fifties or early sixties and pretty well respected by most of her students. She did her best to make English interesting, and though most of us dreaded her classes, we liked her because she always took the time to talk to us and sincerely cared about her students.

"You weren't involved in all that nonsense last Friday night, were you?"

"Naw, not really. Some Panther kids kind of surrounded Jennifer and I—"

"Me," she interrupted. "'Jennifer and me,' Ralph, not 'Jennifer and I.'" She rose from her creaking swivel oak chair to leave for the assembly.

"Yes, ma'am. Anyhow, we were heading to the school bus, and these guys stopped us and took my drumstick and beat me with it. Got my glasses broken, but that was all. That's why I'm wearing these old Buddy Holly frames. I won't get my new ones for a couple of weeks."

"Jennifer didn't get hurt did she?"

"Nope. In fact, she cold-cocked one of the guys with her flute. Knocked him out, I think, then grabbed me and we got right on the bus."

"Good for her," Mrs. Fowler said, nodding her head in approval. "You'd better get along now, to the assembly."

I turned and pushed open the classroom door to the hall. Jennifer was outside waiting for me.

"Old Lady Fowler said this could be a long assembly," I said, putting my arm over and around her shoulders.

"Yeah. Mr. Bamford thought some of the team and other students are gonna be suspended."

The hallway was filled with kids putting books away and slamming locker doors.

When we got into the gym, Slick waved at us from about midway up the center of the bleachers. He was sitting with his girl, Rita Bradley. Rita was a junior cheerleader, blonde, great body, and had one of "those" reputations. Jennifer didn't care for her all that much but got along with her only because Slick was one of my best friends.

A few of the kids were still working their way up the bleachers when Mr. Fluorite tapped the microphone. He then bent down and blew into it, followed by his traditional "Testing. Testing one, two, three." A low squeal screeched from the speakers at the corners of the gym ceiling.

With his hands raised over his head, pushing palms out at us, he said, "Quiet now. Can I have your attention? Please give me your attention."

Some guy toward the back hollered, "NOPE!" and a muffled laughter spread across the bleachers.

Mr. Fluorite turned toward the response, still holding his hands up pushing toward the seated crowd. "I need everybody's undivided attention."

Seated directly behind Fudd, in a row of brown metal folding chairs was Coach Svensen, Daddy Bruce and two other cops, and all seven members of the school board. Sitting at Fudd's right, on the end next to Dr. Holloway, chairman of the school board, was the manager of the Brookshire Hotel, Mr. Fitzgerald. All of them were seated with their legs crossed the exact same direction except Coach Svensen, who was leaning forward with both arms on his legs, his tie dangling loosely between his legs. They all had their heads turned, looking up at Fudd.

"All of you know what this assembly is about. What happened last Friday night after the game was a terrible thing, and that kind of activity will not be tolerated at Pikes Peak High School. I know that not all of you were involved, but this kind of juvenile, even criminal, display of pure stupidity by a very few students has made Pikes Peak High a disgrace to the Brookshire community and the entire city of Colorado Springs. As your principal, as well as a member of this community, I will not tolerate this kind of behavior by the students or anyone else associated with this school. Those few who were involved in the lake incident will be called into my office immediately following this assembly, and they will be dealt with at that time. I will also be talking to other individuals, and if I find out that any others were involved other than those students we already know about, they too will be dealt with at that time.

"I speak not only for myself but for the entire faculty of this institution when I say we're not only disappointed in how this student body conducted themselves at that game, but we're extremely embarrassed. Rather than taking this time to celebrate a great game and victory by our hockey team, we have to hang our heads in shame.

"At this time, I would like Coach Svensen to come up here to say a few words."

By this time little beads of sweat could be seen shining on the top of Fudd's beet-red head. The longer he talked the redder his head got. He turned and moved to one side of the microphone, which squealed again. Coach Svensen put his hands on his knees and stood up, looking down to the floor as he approached the microphone.

The school board, cops, and Mr. Fitzgerald sat like mannequins except to swivel their heads to watch Coach Svensen walk to the mike.

Svensen wasn't a tall man but was built like a weightlifter: broad shoulders and a narrow waist that flared out at his thighs, which were so muscular he couldn't keep his legs together and walked with a stiff swagger. Oddly, though, he didn't have a deep voice to match his stature. Instead, he spoke with a kind of high-pitched voice that he forced as low as he could. We always joked—but never where he could hear us—about his underwear being too tight. He cleared his voice before speaking.

"I would like you all to know that what could have been one of the highlights of the players' and my coaching career has turned into one of the lowest times in my life.

"Over the weekend I was called into a special meeting by the school board. Mr. Fitzgerald was also asked to attend. It was decided, at that time, that the entire Pikes Peak High School hockey program be suspended for a period of one year from today."

A roar of moans and "Noooo"s rumbled throughout the bleachers along with noisy shuffling of feet. Svensen put his hands up in the air to quiet the crowd. It took a few moments before silence returned so the coach could go on.

"That means there will not be a team next year and those of you who are juniors will not be playing hockey during your senior year. And there will not be any practices or team meetings between now and then"—he paused here and cleared his throat—"because the management of the Brookshire Ice Palace and the Brookshire community will not allow our team to practice or participate in any way at their facility for a period of one year from now. As you know, this is the only ice rink in the area, so that settles that."

He turned, walked over to his chair, and sat down.

"Shit! Do you think *we'll* be called into Fudd's office?" Slick leaned over in front of Rita and looked at me. I shrugged my shoulders and never said a word. Fudd stepped back up to the microphone. Except for a few low murmurs it was pretty quiet.

"Unless one of you would like to say something?" Fudd turned to look at the lineup behind him, and all heads were shaking no. He then turned back to the students. "OK. You are dismissed to return to your second-period classes."

Everybody rose and clomped their way down the wooden bleachers, some stomping harder on the wooden planks than normal. Mr. Fluorite was in the center of a huddle of school board members. Daddy Bruce and the other two cops were walking toward the rear entrance to the gym with Mr. Fitzgerald. Coach Svensen was already behind the door to his office on the opposite side of the basketball court.

Slick and I went to Mr. Bamford's chemistry class while Jennifer went to speech and Rita headed to math. Bamford took roll and had started right into his lecture when the intercom from Fudd's office came on. Normally, his secretary, Mrs. Wilson, made any announcements, but now Fudd was on the speaker himself.

"Would the following students report to my office immediately: William Broomfield, Gill Howard, Rick Maloney, Bobby Hunt, Dave Harrison, Jerry Altringer, Jack Petersen, Jim Henry, Walt Greecy, Bill Blackburn, Ralph Jensen, and Dave Harrison."

"You're excused," Bamford said, looking at both Slick and me. We got up and headed for the door. Everybody turned to watch us when Mr. Bamford clapped his hands together. "They've got other things to do, so let me have your attention. Judy, what happens when…"

I didn't hear the rest of the question as the door shut behind me. Other doors were shutting behind other boys leaving classes, also on their way to the principal's office.

Slick and I were walking together when Jerry Altringer caught up to us. "Fuckin' A, if I get suspended my old man will kick the shit out of me."

Slick and I both looked at him and just kept walking. We walked into the main office, and Mrs. Wilson asked us to take a chair. We would be called into Fudd's office one at a time. Altringer was the first to go in, and ten minutes later Fudd escorted him back out. He looked over at Slick and rolled his eyes back while mouthing the words "Ass-hole" and "I'm dead meat."

One at a time we were funneled in and out of Fudd's office. Just before I went in, I saw Jerry come out of the north wing with his jacket on and books under his arm, heading down to the parking lot. "He's a goner," I thought to myself.

"Ralph. Step into my office, please." Fluorite held his door open, stepping to one side as I entered. I sat in one of the two wooden chairs in front of his desk. He sat in his high-backed, padded swivel rocker. "I know you weren't an instigator in the riot last Friday night, and I want to commend you for acting so maturely. However, I know you were involved in a brief scuffle outside the Palace. Therefore, I'm gonna place you on one month's probation, which means that if you get into any other kind of trouble, you will be suspended. Just keep your nose clean and you'll be all right. I know Miss Lucas was also involved, but I am not going to call her in because I understand that she was just trying to help you get to the bus."

"Yes, sir. Jennifer didn't have anything to do with it. Thank you, sir."

"That will be all, Ralph," he said, pushing his chair back and moving around his desk to open the door. He put his hand on my back as I walked past him out the door.

Just as I went out the office door, Slick was coming back out of the north wing. I ran past the library and cut him off before he turned down toward the parking lot to leave.

"What the hell happened?" I asked.

"Fudd suspended my ass for a week. That son-of-a-bitch!" Slick's face was tight, and his eyes went cold. "I don't know what my folks'll do."

I just stood there not knowing what to say.

"I'm on probation for a month. If I screw up in any way, I'll be suspended," I finally said.

All Slick did was give me a little smile and then said, "Good. You lucky bastard."

"If my folks let me out of the house, I'll be down at the Pard tonight around seven. If you can get out I'll see ya there, OK?" I said.

He just shook his head and trotted down the walk, mumbling something I couldn't understand. I turned and headed into the building just as the bell rang to dismiss second period. Jennifer pushed her way through the crowded hallway toward me. I told her what had happened and that everything was fine. We walked to our next class, which we had together.

Chapter *Eight*

When I pulled up to the first speaker at the Pard, the lot was already full of cars and kids were scattered all over in small groups. Apparently Jerry's folks let him out of the house because he was standing next to Slick's car, bent over peering to the driver's side window.

"Can I help you?" Mrs. Harding's voice crackled over the speaker.

"Yup. I'll take a large cherry Coke." I paused. "And that'll do. Thanks."

"Thank you. Please pull forward."

I pulled up to the window and dropped the correct change into Mrs. Harding's hand. She gave me a "thank you" smile and handed me my Coke. I pulled away and turned into the lot, where I drove into a slot next to Slick's Chevy.

When I got out Slick motioned for me to hop in the back. Jerry Altringer was already sitting on the other side of the backseat when I settled in, closing the door behind me.

"Where's Jenny? Got a new beau?" Jerry asked with a cocky grin on his face.

"She had some extra homework to do and couldn't get out of the house tonight," I said. "What'd your folks say when you got home so early from school today? I didn't think we'd see you down here for quite awhile." I brought my drink up and wrapped my lips around the straw and sucked up a cold drink.

"Ah, not much. Actually, my dad kind of surprised me. He was at the game and saw what happened and thought I was just caught up in the middle of the whole mess and couldn't help what happened. In fact, I kinda think he was a little proud of me." Jerry had a bit of a surprised glint to his eyes, and his voice held a sound of pride to it. "He just said I had to live with the consequences and told me to keep my nose clean from here on out. He was also kinda miffed that the Poudre High hockey team wasn't kicked out of the Palace and the league like we were."

"What?! The Panthers can still play next year and practice up at the rink?" My voice was loud and an octave higher than usual.

"Yup. That's what my dad said." Jerry was shaking his head back and forth with both of his hands held flat out, palms up over each shoulder.

"That's also what I heard on the radio," Slick said. "In fact, the news guy even said that the 'lowlands' kids that make up the majority of the Pikes Peak hockey club gave the Brookshire school district a real black eye and he didn't blame the Brookshire for kicking us out of the Ice Palace." Slick emphasized the words "Brookshire" and "Ice Palace" in a la-dee-da tone.

"Those damn Bertha-Better-than-You's—screw 'em! Those snob-nosed bastards!" I was shifting my eyes back and forth quickly between Slick and Jerry, and I could feel the heat of my face turning red. "Hell, they really put our lights out this time. I know you guys were trying hard to get a hockey scholarship to Colorado College, and this just killed your chances for that slicker than shit."

Just about that time my door opened, and Gill Howard nudged me over to the middle of the bench seat. Walt Greecy and Rick Maloney had the right front door open and hopped in next to Slick. Gill was the first to speak.

"Did you guys hear the news about Poudre? Does that suck or what!"

Slick bent down to pull out the cigarette lighter from the dashboard. "Mmmm-mh," he hummed, putting the glowing end of the lighter up to the tip of his Pall Mall, then sucking in to bring it burning to life.

"Give me one of those things." Gill stuck his open hand over toward Slick.

"You don't smoke, Howard!" Rick said.

"I do tonight," Gill replied with a smile on his face. "Light me up."

Gill put the cigarette to his mouth and held it between the center of his lips in a kiddie-kiss pucker. When Slick handed him the lighter, he had to hold the long skinny paper tube with his other hand in order to hit the end with the lighter. He made a few quick popping sounds with his lips as he sucked in and blew out great clouds of blue smoke that hovered around his head, quickly filling the entire cab of Slick's Chevy. His fourth puff was followed by a series of hacking coughs before he put the butt back to his lips and started puffing on it again.

"Jesus, Gill, either learn how to smoke that thing or put it out," I said, leaning over Gill's lap to roll down the window. By this time all of us were waving our hands in front of our faces, trying to clear a clean spot of air to breathe. Gill just laughed, coughed, puffed, laughed, and coughed again.

Slick turned to face Gill and pointed at his own cigarette, which was hanging from the corner of his mouth. "Like this." Slick sucked on his cigarette, making the end glow, and took the butt from his mouth holding it between the index and middle fingers of his left hand. His mouth opened slightly and the thick smoke curled out, trying to escape just before it vanished in a rush down Slick's throat. Ever so easily he formed his lips into a loose oval shape, tipped his head back slightly, and exhaled. A much thinner current of smoke came rushing back out, gliding along the cloth liner of the car roof before circling back and out the window behind Gill.

"Sure. No sweat. I can do that." Gill put the butt to his mouth, took a hefty drag, let the smoke curl out of his mouth, and with a gasp inhaled as hard as he could. I don't think the thick cloud of smoke made it down to his Adam's apple before his eyes opened wide and he started gagging and coughing his guts out. Tears came to his eyes, and he instantly turned pale as a sheet. Still sputtering he managed to speak in a squeally voice, "Gawd damn—*cough*—that's good shit—*cough, cough, wheeze. I'll*—*cough, wheeze*—get it right—*cough*—just—*cough*—watch."

He took another drag, and I can't tell you for sure what happened because I was laughing (and coughing from the smoke) so hard just like everybody else.

"One thing's for sure—you guys don't have to worry about Svensen catching you smoking or drinking and kicking you off the team. Hell, you can even slam back a few suds with no sweat," I said, taking off my glasses to wipe the tears from my eyes from laughing so hard.

"I'm gonna die if I don't get out of here!" Rick opened his door and bailed out. Jerry and I went out Jerry's side, and even Slick rolled out of the driver's side. A second later Gill staggered out of the car, throwing the butt to the ground. "Man, am I dizzy." He walked a few uneasy steps to my car and put both of his hands on the roof and hung his head between them. "Jesus, Slick, how can you stand those things? *Cough, cough, cough.*" Then he wandered off, walking in a small circle, trying to regain his breath and balance.

"It takes a real man," Slick laughed.

"Screw you and the horse you rode in on," Gill coughed.

Slick just looked at Gill, lifted his cigarette to his mouth, took another long, easy drag, inhaling with no problem, and stuck his lower lip out and up, blowing the smoke out and up in front of his face. Gill wandered back and leaned one hand on the trunk of Old Ironsides and slowly raised his other hand, flipping Slick the bird. All of us broke out again in uncontrolled laughter.

"What the heck is going on over here? Looks like Gill's gonna get sick and you guys think that's funny?"

Howie Jones was pointing at Gill and had a "let me in on the joke" look on his face. Jim Henry and Dave Harrison were right behind Howie, heading over to join us. Howie was the first-chair trumpet player for our pep band and always hung around with Jim and Dave. He could have easily played football or hockey, but his folks didn't want him in any sports because they thought he might get hurt. He was well built and always hung around with the rest of the jocks. If there was a fight, he was always in the middle of the action, and most of us considered him the bully of the school. I always thought he acted that way to try to prove to everyone he wasn't a pussy.

Even though Jim Henry played on the hockey team, he was kind of a string-bean and never made first string. In a strange way he was trying to prove his manhood just like Howie.

Dave Harrison was the tag-a-long with these two and would do most anything they told him to do. Dave was a nice enough guy but just wasn't real bright. Most everybody called him by his nickname, Zero. He got tagged with "Zero" by the football coach because he knew only one play, which they called "zero" in the playbook. As the fullback, he'd get sent in for all the short-yardage plays, and all the opposing coaches would know exactly what was happening the minute Zero was sent onto the field. The quarterback would simply hand the ball off to Dave, and he would crash his way straight up the middle. With his six-two, 240-pound bulk of solid muscle, he'd slumber up to the line with his head down and the football safely cradled in his arms, then crash his way up the field for two or three yards—even with half the opposing team grabbing hold of him. He'd mow 'em over just like bowling pins until the sheer weight of the clasping bodies pulled him to the ground. One time, when we played the team from the southeastern Colorado town of Lamar, Zero actually broke through their line and was in the open. When he realized he was free and still standing, he stopped and looked back at the pile of players behind him while the coach and all of us were screaming and shouting at the top of our lungs, "RUN, RUN, RUN!" He looked over at us as if to say, "Oh, yeah," then turned and lumbered on down the field for the fifteen remaining yards for a touchdown. His fantastic finish won the game for the Indians, and he was the hero of the week. And he thought he was the hero of the week every week after that game.

Gill regained his equilibrium and breath, and Slick went over to pat him on the back. "Old Gill here just wasn't cut out to smoke like a man." "You pussy," said Henry.

Everybody kind of split up into two groups—half of us leaning up against Old Ironsides and the rest leaning up against Slick's Chevy, facing each other. Jim and Zero each had a can of Coors and Howie was sucking on a cup of pop.

"We were just talking," Jerry said, "about how we should do something to those damn Brookshire do-gooders for kickin' our asses off of their high and mighty hill." He pointing toward the Brookshire.

Walt Greecy hadn't said a word up until this point. "Why don't we form a gang and make a plan?"

Silence followed his statement as we all looked at him and then at each other. The silence was broken with a series of "yeah"s and "sounds cool to me."

Altringer was the only one who hesitated. "I don't know, guys. If I get in any more trouble, my old man will kick my butt from here to Kansas."

"Hell, Jer, we're all in that boat," Slick said. "We can't just sit around here and not do nothin' at all. If they don't want us up there, we sure as hell don't want them down here. Let's join together and do something."

"Cool, man. Let's go!" Zero turned to leave, not knowing for sure where he was going so he quickly turned around and stepped back into the group.

"First, we've got to agree that we're a gang that will stick together and make a plan of attack," Rick Maloney said, holding a clenched fist out and swinging it in everyone's direction.

"Cool. Let's meet down here at seven o'clock this Friday night and do it." Slick held his hand out and I shook it, then we all criss-crossed over and above each other's arms and sealed the deal with everybody's handshake. The first gang in the history of Pikes Peak High School was now official.

Chapet *Nine*

North Cheyenne Canyon was considered Lover's Lane for the Pikes Peak rich kids. Where you entered the canyon, the road split into a Y, and if you turned to the left you would drive up South Cheyenne Canyon to the world-famous Seven Falls tourist attraction. The short drive is billed as one of the most scenic in the country with sheer granite cliffs rising skyward along both rims of the canyon. Thousands of people drive up to see the falls each summer during the tourist season. They even light the falls up at night, using different colors during the Christmas holiday season.

Parallel to both canyon roads were two tiny creeks, each named for the canyons they descended, North Cheyenne Creek and South Cheyenne Creek respectively. The creeks met at the mouth of each canyon and became a single flowing stream simply known as Cheyenne Creek. The creek flowed eastward right along the base of the hill, forming a natural border between Brookshire and the lowlands.

Penrose Boulevard came off of Highway 85, which headed south out of the Springs toward Canon City, some fifty miles to the south. The total distance from the mouth of the canyons to the highway was some eight miles. In order to get up to Brookshire from either the lowlands or the Springs, you had to cross one of four wooden bridges over the creek. One of these bridges crossed over the creek about a quarter of a mile east of the mouth of the canyons. The other three bridges crossed the creek at two-mile intervals downstream until you hit Highway 85.

The bridge near the canyon crossed the creek on Seven Falls Road. Two miles downstream you crossed over the Stover Road Bridge. The next entrance to Brookshire was over the Will Rogers Bridge, and the fourth access bridge took you up the hill via Alsace Way.

Penrose Boulevard was the main entrance to the Brookshire community and headed west off Highway 85 straight as an arrow. From the minute you got on Penrose Boulevard from the highway, you could see the Brookshire Hotel towering above the far end of the road where the boulevard ended in the cul-de-sac entrance to the hotel.

Seven Falls Road was used mainly by Brookshire guests on their way up to see the falls. Stover Road and Alsace Way were used mostly by residents of the Brookshire community as they traveled to and from the lowlands area and downtown Colorado Springs. Will Rogers Road was the main thoroughfare leading up to the hotel from the Springs.

All of these access roads intersected with Cheyenne Road, which paralleled the north side of the creek along the entire distance from the mouth of the canyons east to Highway 85. The only way anyone could drive up to or out of Brookshire was across one of these four wooden bridges or west off of Highway 85 on Penrose Boulevard, which also crossed over a wooden bridge that spanned a dry gulch just before it intersected the highway. There weren't any roads leading south out of Brookshire.

It was Wednesday evening at about seven when I swung by Jennifer's house to pick her up. Ever since we started going together during our junior year, we saved Wednesday evenings as a special date night for ourselves. Because she had to be home by nine o'clock on school nights, we usually headed over to the Pard to hang out, cruised Nevada Avenue, the main drag dissecting the heart of the Springs from north to south, or we headed up to North Cheyenne Canyon to park for an hour or so, which was tonight's plan.

I turned Old Ironsides south on Eighth Street to Cheyenne Road, made a right turn, and headed west toward the north canyon. About three miles up the winding canyon road, we came to our special spot. I pulled off the pavement onto a narrow gravel road that wound three hundred feet through towering Ponderosa pines down to the edge of the creek. I never told Jennifer that I had taken two previous girlfriends to this same spot; she thought it was found exclusively by us.

Even though the temperature outside was only in the mid-thirties, I rolled down the window on my side just a crack and turned off the car, turning the key around to auxiliary so we could listen to the radio. We always listened to the local rock-n-roll station KYSN until eight o'clock, when we switched over to KOMA out of Oklahoma City. KYSN was a good station and played all of our favorite tunes, but at eight KOMA increased their wattage and also carried the howling Wolfman Jack.

Tonight the KYSN deejay was announcing three in a row, leading off with Elvis Presley's "Jailhouse Rock," followed by Bobby Darin's "Mack the Knife," with the third song—and our favorite—"Mr. Blue," crooned by Bobby Vinton.

It was one of those perfectly clear November Colorado nights, and the stars glistened like a zillion fireflies high above the tall pine trees. I put my arm around Jennifer's shoulders, pulling her around to me as I moved my feet over the hump in the middle of the floor over to her side of the car and slid down against my door. Jennifer bent her legs up and pushed her feet across the front seat and against the passenger door. She scooted up across my chest until her face was equal with mine. We had done this many times before and eased into a comfortable position. I put my left hand under her chin and cupped her face in the palm of my hand, lightly drawing her lips down to mine. My other hand worked its way up under her light jacket pulling her blouse out from the waistband of her skirt. As soon as it was free my hand felt the smooth warmth of her skin. She had her arms around my back and pulled me into her. She made a faint humming moan when I snaked my tongue into her mouth and fenced with hers. My left hand found the three-in-a-row hooks on the back strap of her bra, and I popped all three with three quick flicks of my index finger and thumb. Pressing her lips harder on mine, she lifted up slightly so I could ease my hand up between us, push her bra up, and cup her firm left breast. The nipple sprung out taut to my touch. "And this one's for all you young lovers out there steamin' up the car windows," the KYSN deejay said, and Vinton's voice filled the car with "I'm Mr. Blue..."

"What are you guys gonna do Friday?" Jennifer was lifting herself up and pushing her shoulders back against the top of the seat, tucking her blouse back into her skirt. Her eyes were glassy with unfulfilled satisfaction and looking straight into mine. I still had my arm over her shoulders, and when she was finished rearranging her clothes, I pulled her back into me. Both of us turned and looked up through the foggy windshield at the blurry stars.

"I don't know for sure." I kept looking up at the stars.

"Do I get to go along or is this just for a bunch of you guys?" She turned her head toward me and looked into my eyes.

"I don't think this will be the kind of gang girls would want to be a part of, and I don't want you to get into any trouble."

"Ralph, I don't want you to get into any trouble, either—or hurt. You won't do anything stupid or dangerous will you? When all of you guys get together, I know anything goes."

I looked up through the windshield. "All I know is the Brookshire snobs don't want us up there. They didn't do a thing to the Panthers, and *they* were the ones who started the fight. You saw it when their entire bench flipped us off. They don't want to see us up there, and we don't want to see them down here."

I brought my arm quickly back from around Jennifer's shoulders and bolted straight up in my seat. "I've got it! I know what we're gonna do! I've got it!"

Jennifer snapped up and moved a little bit away from me, putting one hand on the dashboard and the other over the top of the seat, bent at the elbow and turning to face me. "Got what? What are you talking about?"

She quickly brought both of her hands up to her head, grasping a barrette with one hand and holding another between her lips. She brushed the hair on that side of her head back and replaced the barrette. She repeated the process on the other side, until her hair looked exactly like it did when we'd first arrived at our parking spot.

"We'll black out Brookshire! I know Jerry, Rick, Slick, and Zero have pellet guns or .22 rifles. I don't know if anybody else has a gun, but I've got a couple and someone can use one of mine. Operation Black Out Brookshire! We'll shoot out every damn streetlight up there, and they won't be able to see their hands in front of their faces. They don't want to see us up there? Well, we don't want to see them up there, either. Operation Black Out Brookshire is perfect and we can do it."

"Shoot out all the streetlights?! With guns?!" Jennifer looked right at me and bounced back across the seat toward her door. "You're nuts, Ralph!"

"Yeah. But. Jesus, it'll be cool."

I reached down for the keys on the steering column and turned them, bringing Ironsides to life. I turned around, putting my right arm over the backseat and craned my neck to look through the back window. With Ironsides in reverse, I slowly backed up the gravel road and onto the pavement, cranking the steering wheel hard to swing us around so we could head back down the canyon.

"We've got to head for home so you're not late, and I want to call all the guys to set up a meeting tomorrow night at the Pard. They're gonna flip out when I tell them my plan of attack."

Jennifer slid back over next to me and put her left hand up to the back of my neck, lightly scratching her fingers up and down along my hairline. As we were making the last turn before heading out of the canyon I had to brake for a four-point mule deer buck that bounced across the road in front of us.

"Have a good evening, Charley," Jennifer said to the buck as he disappeared into the darkness. We saw that muley buck almost every time we went up there, and Jennifer had given him the name Charley.

Chapter *Ten*

When I turned off of Eighth Street into the Pard, Jerry's and Rick's cars were already parked over in the far corner of the lot. There weren't any cars in the drive-up lane, so I pulled right up to the Pard's pick-up window. Mrs. Harding opened the window and took my order for a cherry Coke. She handed it out the window, and I gave her the exact change.

"How are you doin' tonight, Ralph?"

"Just fine, Mrs. Harding. Thanks," I said, nodding good-bye, and pulled away to join Jerry and Rick across the lot.

"Where're the rest of the guys? I thought we were all together on this gang thing," I said, hopping out of my car.

"Take it easy, Rock—they'll all be here. In fact, here comes Bobby now." Rick made a casual gesture toward the entrance to the Pard.

"What's this big plan of yours, anyway?" Rick's voice held a bit of sarcasm to it.

"You guys will love it, and I'll let you know as soon as the rest of the gang shows up," I said.

Just as Bobby's car pulled up next to Ironsides, Gill was turning into the lot, and right behind him was the dynamic trio: Howie, Jim, and Zero. They all got out of their cars and walked around to join us where we were standing between Ironsides and Rick's Ford Fairlane.

"Here comes Gill, and it looks like Greecy is with him," Howie said, leaning up against Ironsides. "Jerry called me just before I left and told me he'd be a little late but would get here as soon as he could. What's up?" Jim and Zero followed suit, plopping up against my car right nest to Howie like his faithful followers.

"Yeah, what's up?" Zero echoed.

"Operation Black Out Brookshire." There was a dull silence when I announced the title of my plan. Quizzical looks came from everyone.

"What are you talking about, Rock?" Rick looked around and spoke for everyone.

I leaned forward off of the car and put my arms out with the fingers of each hand spread out. I can't exactly say there was a resounding shout of enthusiasm as I started to lay out my plan of attack on Brookshire.

"Now, I know Rick and Zero have pellet guns and Slick has a .22 rifle—" Before I could continue, Howie and Jim shouted in unison, "GUNS!"

"What the hell are we gonna do with guns?" Howie asked. "Charge up the hill with guns blazing? Rocky, you've gotta be crazier than a goddamn loon!"

"No. Now wait a minute and listen to me." I pumped both of my hands up and down in an attempt to calm everybody so I could explain my plan.

"Shit, Rock, you're nuts!" Gill said, shaking his head and starting to head back to his car.

Nobody saw Jerry's car come into the lot. Slick was already parked down the way, and they both were coming around Rick's car when they heard Gill shouting at me,

"What the hell's going on? We just get here and it sounds like our gang's breaking up before we even get started. Come on, you guys, let's at least hear what Rock has to say about his plan before we all jump on him."

"Guns! Jesus, you guys, he wants to use guns. He's crazier than hell, and I don't want any part of that shit." Walt was turning around to leave with Gill.

"Wait a minute! Wait a minute, guys! I don't want to shoot anybody. I just want to go up there and shoot every one of their fuckin' street-lights out. Operation Black Out Brookshire. Get it? We need .22 rifles or pellet guns to do that. You've got a .22, don't you, Slick?" He shook his head yes. "Besides, it'll be a big kick in the ass." I was talking fast and trying to make my idea hit home before everybody told me to go to hell.

"Shoot out *every* streetlight? That's cool. That's really cool. We could do it!" Everybody turned toward Slick. "All we need to do is map out a plan that will work."

Walt and Gill returned to the huddle. "OK, Slick," Gill said, "I'll listen to Rock's idea. But, Christ, do we have to use guns?" Walt shook his head in questioning agreement with Gill.

"Just cool your shorts and let's hear what he has to say," Slick replied. "If anybody doesn't want to go along with Rock's plan, they can leave. No hard feelings. That OK with you, Rock? Is everybody else cool?" Slick looked around the group, then centered on me. "Well, let's hear it."

I looked over at Slick and gave him a quick thank-you gesture and started to walk slowly into the center of the huddle. In a slight crouch that expressed my excitement, I glided around in front of each one of them. "We can do this, you guys. All we need to do is organize ourselves into four separate groups. Brookshire is mapped out perfectly for my plan. Penrose Boulevard splits the whole area exactly down the middle from east to west, and Will Rogers divides Brookshire in half from north to south." I paused, stepped back, and looked around. "OK so far?" Heads nodded in agreement. "Now," I continued, "if we all assign one driver with a shooter to each quarter section of the Hill, we could shoot out every streetlight in each section in a couple of hours, tops."

Jerry stepped in front of me. "Wait a minute, Rock. Did the thought ever occur to you that some of those folks up there might not like the idea of a bunch of teenagers with guns running around their streets and blasting away at their streetlights in the middle of the night? Did that ever cross your mind? I mean, like, hey man, they're gonna call old Daddy Bruce the second they hear the first shot, and he's gonna come down on us like fresh horse shit. What in hell are we gonna do about him?"

"Yup. We'd be dead meat in no time flat." All of us looked at Zero in amazement when he spoke.

"Zero's right. Unless we figure out a way to corral ol' Daddy, we're dead before we even get started," Jim said, looking down and kicking his foot back and forth through the gravel, already defeated.

"Hey! Jim's exactly right!" shouted Bobby Hunt. "We need to corral that old bastard, and I know exactly how we can do it." Bobby quickly moved into the center of the circle, slowly spinning around and pointing his finger at no one in particular. He tipped back his Sky Socks baseball cap to just above his hairline, eyes intense with excitement. "You know that polo field off of Blue Spruce Drive, just a couple of blocks east of the hotel and a block north of Penrose Boulevard? It has two huge steel gates. One on the east side and one at the west side of the field, and both of them run right along Blue Spruce."

"Big deal, Bobby," Zero snickered. "What do you think we'll do—trap Daddy in the polo field?"

"Not exactly, but you are damn close to being right, Zero." Bobby pulled his cap back down hard over his eyebrows. "If you guys remember, when they swing both of those gates all the way out, they stretch completely across Blue Spruce, and they're chained to those two huge pine trees on the other side of the street across from each gate. Because of the big stone fences along the front yards of those two estates on the other side of the street, nobody can get into—or out of—the field when they're using it."

"That'll work, Bobby." Slick bounced into the center of the circle with Bobby.

"Damn right it will," Bobby said, taking over the conversation again. "All we have to do is figure out how to get ol' Daddy in there."

"Yeah, but what about those two side-kick deputies?" Zero asked.

The excitement that had started to bring the gang together was slacking off quickly.

"All except one of his deputies go off duty after ten." All of us turned around at the new sound of Bill Blackburn's voice. "Daddy Bruce and one deputy are the only ones who work after ten o'clock on Friday and Saturday nights."

Even though Bill was a senior at Pikes Peak High, he never had a steady clique that he hung around with. He was one of those do-gooder kind of kids who got great grades and never got into any kind of trouble. Because he was going with Jeannie Fitzgerald, he was accepted by the Brookshire folks as one of their own; Jeannie's being the daughter of the hotel's manager didn't hurt. They'd been a couple ever since their freshmen year and both had plans to go to the University of Colorado that next fall. Marriage was also rumored to be part of their plans in the near future.

"Hey, Bill! What the hell you doin' here?" I said, looking quickly around the group, hoping they'd catch the glint in my eyes to shut up.

Everybody clammed up, and the tension could be felt in the air. The last thing we needed right now was for our gang to get busted before we even did anything. We all started to mill around in an uneasy fashion."Don't sweat it, fellas. I'm not gonna squeal on you about your gang or anything you've got planned."

"Yeah, sure, Sweet William. Hey, guys, Mister Goody-Two-Shoes wasn't gonna say a thing about our plan to black out—"

"Shut up, Zero!" Slick grabbed Zero by the shoulder and pulled him back, giving him an "or else" scowl. Zero moved behind Slick, looking over his shoulder.

Bill stood his ground and then took another step into the edge of the broken circle. "If you guys are planning on doing anything up Brookshire way, I'd like to join you."

"Slick," Zero whined, "we can't trust this son-of-a-bitch. Hell, he's slept with one of their slimy bitches."

Bill Blackburn may not have been one of the top athletes at Pikes Peak High, but his six-foot frame was backed up by a solid build from hard work on his dad's ranch up near Cripple Creek. Because of Pikes Peak High's reputation, his folks owned a home in the lowlands so their kids could go to school down there during the school year. When summer came, they moved back up to the ranch. Bill had an easy-going temper, but Zero's crass reference to Jeannie set him off, and he reached out, pushing Slick aside. Zero stepped back and brought up both fists, ready to defend himself, but he was too late. Bill grabbed Zero's left arm and twisted it back and behind him. He had Zero's other arm before Zero could do anything to defend himself. He slammed Zero hard into the side of Old Ironsides. In the slow drawl of a Hollywood cowboy, Bill said, "Her name is Jeannie, asshole, and if you say another word about anything while I'm here, your asshole will sport a new set of teeth. Get it?" He slammed Zero up hard against the car again. "Get it?" With Bill forcing Zero's own arm into his Adam's apple, Zero couldn't speak, so he nodded slightly in agreement. With another strong shove, Bill then eased back and let Zero loose. As soon as Bill turned back toward us, Zero stepped up and was going to hit him in the back of the head, but Slick's hand moved over quickly behind Bill and caught Zero's fist before it connected.

"You are one slow-learner, Zero," Slick said. "Blackburn could whip your butt with no sweat. And, when he was finished with you, I'd take over. Now stand there and shut up." Slick turned back around. "Now, cool it, everyone—just cool it. Let's hear what Bill has to say." Zero moved over behind Howie and Jim, looking hard at Blackburn, and then quickly glanced down to his feet.

Just as if nothing had happened, Bill looked around at us, "Hey, fellas, I don't want to cause any more trouble. I just wanted to help out if I could. See ya later." Bill walked between us and headed over to his blue Ford pickup.

"Wait up!" Walt called out. "Come on back. Zero really didn't mean anything. You know how he is. Besides, not all of us feel that way, do we, fellas?" Walt caught up with Bill and put his hand on his shoulder, turning him around.

In a mumbled chorus a weak voice of unity said, "Naw, let's hear what you have to say." Walt took his hand off Bill's shoulder, and they slowly rambled back, with Walt trailing behind and herding Bill back into the circle.

"We just always thought you were one of them more than one of us because of Jeannie," I said.

He looked me right in the eye and snarled, "Just leave her outta this, Rock. She has nothin' to do with it."

"OK. Fine with me." I put both of my hands up in front of me, both palms facing outward, and backed away. I didn't want any part of Bill.

Slick stepped up. "What are you doing here, anyway? You don't have a gripe against the hill."

"You guys won't believe what happened," Bill said, and settled in against the side of Rick's car. "Because of what happened the other night after the game up at the Palace, Jeannie's old man decided it would be better for both of us if we stopped seeing each other."

"You gotta be shittin' me!" Zero burst out. He must have had a lapse of memory about his previous agreement a few seconds before with Bill to keep quiet. Bill stared right into him, and Zero moved back behind Jim and Howie. Slick quickly put an "easy, now" hand on Bill's shoulder and eased him back against the car.

"Mr. Fitzgerald said he didn't want any problems to come up that Jeannie couldn't handle, bein's how I'm not from the Hill and all. Just thought it'd be better for the both of us. And, when I asked him what

Jeannie thought about his ideas he said it doesn't really concern her. When I asked to see her, he just told me to go home, and then he shut the door." Bill quit talking, looked around, then shrugged his shoulders.

"Fuckin' A. If that don't beat all." Howie moved over to Bill and put his hand on his shoulder. "If Bill wants to be a part of our gang, it's all right with me."

"Yeah. Me too. Me too." A unanimous acceptance was echoed around the circle.

Zero looked at Bill and quietly said, "Me too."

Bill smiled.

I moved back into the center of the circle. "We were just putting together our plan for Operation Black Out Brookshire. This is what we've decided to do so far."

"I heard some of it before I came over, and I don't think this is a very good place to talk about anything we're gonna do," Bill said with a slight nod of his head indicating for us to look around. "Too many ears around this place."

All of us looked around and turned back to Bill. "I know a perfect place up South Cheyenne Canyon, along the Gold Camp Road," he said. "It's called Hucky Cove. It's a cave in the side of the mountain that hardly anybody knows about. With a few Coleman lanterns, some chairs, and a table, it could work as the gang's headquarters."

We were all looking at each other, waiting for somebody to say something when Slick spoke up. "Let's go take a look."

"We'll have to wait until this weekend and go up there when it's light enough to see," Bill said. "We can use my pickup to haul the table and chairs, plus anything else we need to set up camp."

"I can get an old card table and chairs, plus a lantern," I said.

Howie raised his hand. "I'll bring a couple of extra chairs and another lantern. And, hey, Bobby, your folks still want to get rid of that old sofa?"

"Yup."

"Great! Bring what you can, and let's meet at that first picnic area at the mouth of the canyon next Saturday morning at nine sharp," I said, "Let's do it!"

Chapter *Eleven*

I pulled Ironsides into the picnic area about a quarter to nine. Bill was already there, standing against the tailgate of his truck with the heel of one cowboy boot raised up and hooked onto the ridge of the bumper. He was reaching into a small can of Skoal, picking out a pinch of the fine-ground tobacco to put under his lower front lip. The pressure of the lump of chew against his lower front teeth made his lower lip bulge out like he had a small marble behind his lip. His beat-up old black Stetson was cocked back on his head. Blue faded Levis, a checkered western shirt with pearl buttons snapped up the front to an open collar, and a well-worn fleece-lined Lee jean jacket loosely hanging from his broad shoulders rounded out his appearance. Replacing the lid on the can of chew and tucking it back into his rear pocket, he acknowledged my arrival with a slight nod of his head.

"Got here early, huh? How long you been here?" I asked, slamming my door and walking around the back of Ironsides to join Bill against his tailgate.

"Yup. Been here ten minutes or so," he replied, spitting a long stream of brown juice, hitting a small rock I'm sure he was aiming at. "Just wanted to get this gang put together and get on with it. Bring anything we need to put in the truck?"

I pushed myself away from the tailgate and went over to pop the trunk on Ironsides. "Just brought a card table and four old metal folding chairs."

I lifted Ironside's trunk lid open to show Bill.

"May as well load all that stuff in the back of my truck. We can just leave your car here if you want and you can ride up to the cove with me."

"OK. Sounds good to me." I reached into the trunk and grabbed the table. Bill lowered the tailgate and sauntered over to pick up two of the steel chairs in each hand. We carried them over to his truck and plopped everything onto the bed, pushing them forward to the front end.

Bill got up into the bed of the truck and snugged the folded table and chairs into one corner. Both of us turned around at the sound of other cars turning into the picnic area.

Bobby was the first one to pull up. He turned his car around and backed up to the back end of Bill's truck. He had an old beaten-up, tan vinyl couch sticking out of the trunk of his car. It was tied down with a spider web of clothesline rope. Each little bump he hit while backing up made the couch teeter up and down, looking like it was defying all the laws of gravity. It was a pure miracle he made it this far without losing it.

"Better haul it up to the cove in your truck, Bill. I don't think it will go any further riding like this," Bobby hollered out, his head out the window looking back at us.

Howie came in right behind Bobby, and we transferred the overstuffed chair he had in his trunk onto the truck. By the time we put everything into Bill's truck that would fit, we were ready to head for our new hideout.

I hopped into the passenger's side of Bill's truck. Immediately the smell of ranch and country hit me. The truck cabin held the odors of cow manure and horse. The seat was covered with a southwestern Indian-designed, cloth strap-on seat cover. Stretched across the back window was a rubber-coated steel gun rack that had three hooks to hold as many guns. Instead of guns hanging on the hooks, Bill's dress Stetson and a rain slicker hung from one side, and directly behind him on the driver's side was a loosely coiled, braided lariat that showed a lot of use. When I withdrew my hand from bracing myself on the dashboard as I got in, my handprint was left in the thick dust. Bill turned the key to start the engine, and I could hear the faint hum of his radio warming up. KYOT was the local country-western station, and when the radio finally powered up, George Jones was right in the middle of "The Race Is On."

"Don't mind listenin' to a little country do you, Rock." It wasn't a question, just a courtesy, and I shook my head in a "not at all" manner. When we turned the truck up the canyon, I leaned forward to get the right angle on the side mirror outside my door. Our gang was on the move as we snaked our way up the canyon.

Close to ten miles up the North Cheyenne Canyon, the road came to an end at Helen Hunt Falls, where a little curio shop stood at the base of the falls and at the head of a short trail that wound up the mountain to the top of the falls. The curio shop was boarded up for the winter and wouldn't reopen until next year's Mother's Day weekend, which was the traditional beginning of the tourist season. The falls were named after the woman who wrote "America the Beautiful." She was inspired by the vast beauty she saw from up here looking down across the foothills of the Rockies and across the Great American Plains to the east.

From the curio shop's small parking lot, the paved road ended, turning to gravel after making a sharp U-turn. A half-mile of tight switchbacks later, the road intersected with Gold Camp Road. Turning right at the intersection would take you out along the Gold Camp Road, which skirted the foothills from there north, overlooking the Springs until it dropped down from the mountains to the abandoned gold smelting plant on the west edge of the Springs.

We turned right, heading west into the heart of the Pikes Peak range. If you stayed on this road, it would eventually take you directly into the Cripple Creek gold-mining district sixty-five miles to the west.

"Hucky Cove is just a mile or so more. We'll be there in a minute." These were the first words Bill said since we left the picnic area.

Sure enough, a mile or so down the road Bill turned onto a rough, rocky road a couple hundred yards, leading right up to the mouth of what looked like an entrance to a cave. The cars behind us followed right along as though Bill's truck were a mama quail. The area directly in front of the cave was just large and flat enough for everybody to park their cars.

Within minutes we were all out of our cars and heading for the mouth of the cave. Slick fired up one of his lanterns, and we headed into the cave, following Bill, who held the lantern high enough so all of us could see where we were going.

"My folks used to take us up here to play every so often, and I've also had a picnic or two here with Jeannie," Bill said, leading us in to the darkness.

Zero started to say something smart, but Jerry elbowed him quick and hard in the ribs. A loud "oomph" was all we heard.

As soon as we entered the cave, the musty smell of cold, damp granite filled our nostrils. Other than a few scattered rocks here and there, the floor was smooth. The entrance was narrow, forcing us into single file for fifty feet, and then the cave opened up into a huge oval room twenty or thirty feet wide and a good fifty feet long, with a flat floor and a high ceiling that soaked up the light from the lantern, making it almost impossible to see the ceiling. When someone spoke, their words held a hollow echo that didn't last long, as if the walls of the cove swallowed up the noise.

"This is scary. Let's get outta here!" Zero's voice quivered when he spoke, and he started to push his way back through the group, heading toward the entrance. He stopped when I said, "Bill, this is cool! It'll be perfect. Let's go back outside and start hauling the stuff in."

Slick took over the command and started ordering everybody around: "Bill, you stay here with the lantern. Jerry, go out and get the other lanterns, light 'em and bring 'em back in here so we can see what we're doing. Get a stick or something that we can stick in the wall to hang a light on. Get movin'."

All of us scampered back outside and started hauling everything inside the cave. We placed the card table and four chairs in the center of the room and put one of the lanterns in the middle of the table. In half an hour we had everything inside the cave and arranged all around the room. With more light, Zero became more comfortable, but he was ready to bolt right out of there in a flash if anything went wrong. Even with more light, his eyes were as wide as he could get them.

We were all sitting either on a rock, one of the chairs, or on the sofa, admiring our new home away from home and the new headquarters for the gang. After a few minutes I stood up and said, "Let's put our plan together so we can kick in Operation Black Out Brookshire tonight."

Chapter *Twelve*

The burnt fumes of white gas from the lanterns was intermingling with the musty odor of the damp cave. There was a slight passing of air moving from the entrance into and out of the cave, so the flames in the lanterns were constantly flickering. Between the cones of heat rising from each lantern and our own body heat, the temperature in the cave rose to where it was comfortable enough for us to take off our jackets. Other than the light given off by the lanterns, the only other bright spot came from a glow of sunshine reflecting off the walls around the entrance from the sunlight coming into the cave's entrance. I was standing over the card table, where I had a road map of the Brookshire community unfolded and laid out.

"Come on over and gather around the table, and I'll show you my plan."

Slick moved over to my right side and Bill stood to my right. The rest of the gang moved in close around the table, except for Zero, who stepped a little closer but held his ground midway between us and the exit. The lantern's light threw upward shadows across everyone's faces, radiating a ghoulish appearance to all the faces looking down at the map.

Smoothing the map's creases with the fingers of my left hand, I pointed to the division lines separating Brookshire into four equal quadrants with my right hand. "What I've done is divide Brookshire into four basic quadrants dissected east to west by Penrose Boulevard and north to south by Will Rogers road." I looked up and around to the glowing faces to see if there were any questions. "To simplify everything, I assigned two guys to a car and each one of those cars to a specific quadrant. Each team will be responsible for shooting out every—and I mean *every*—streetlight in your assigned quadrant. There is one light on each corner of every block—"

"That'll be impossible, Rock," Maloney interrupted, looking from the map to me. "There must be at least a couple hundred lights in each one of those quadrants. It'll take forever, and we won't have enough time to get 'em all and still get away."

"Cool it, Rick. I've got it all figured out and nobody will get caught if all of us stick to the plan."

Nobody was smiling. Every facial expression was serious. Slick looked up at Rick and glanced around at the rest of the gang. "Let Rock finish," he said. "Shit, I *know* we can make this thing work."

"OK, now listen up." I moved my fingers along both Penrose Boulevard and Will Rogers Road, which separated quadrant number one from the rest of the map, and looked over at Slick and Jerry. "You two will be in charge of covering this area to the southeast. Rick, you'll be the shooter and Slick will drive his car, OK?" They both looked at me, then at each other, and nodded their mutual approval.

"Quadrant number two will be covered by Howie and Jim." I moved my right hand along the borders defining quadrant two to the southwest.

Before Howie and Jim could respond, Zero stepped up to the table, butting in between Gill and Howie. "Wait a minute. I want to go with my buddies. Howie, Jim, and me always do everything together, and I won't go with nobody else." Zero slammed his fist down hard on the table almost knocking over the lantern. Bill grabbed the base of the lantern, keeping it upright. The movement of the shaking lantern sent eerie shadows slithering in all directions over and along the uneven granite walls and ceiling of the cave.

"Zero! Cool it, Goddamn it!" Howie grabbed him by both shoulders and pushed him back away from the table "Rock's not leaving you out, you dumb shit. Besides, if you keep acting like an asshole, I'm not sure Jim and I *want* you in on this with us."

"Boy, that's for damn sure." Jim looked over at Zero, shaking his head back and forth.

I stood up straight, looking right at Zero. "Zero! I've got something special I want you to do, and you'll be working with your two buddies." I glanced over their way with a questioning look in my eyes, then turned back to Zero. "If it's all right with Jim and Howie. But if you don't cool it and quit being a big pain in the ass, we'll kick your butt right out of this gang. I mean it, Zero. Got it?" I looked him hard right in the eyes and leaned over, pushing my finger hard into his chest. I quickly looked around at the rest of the guys, and we all shifted our eyes directly back at Zero, isolating him with our stern glares.

"OK. OK. I'm with you all the way." Zero stiffened up, squared his shoulders, then slouched his body into a giving-in stance, walked over and plopped down on the couch. The cushion he sat on let out a forced flutter of air, sounding like a long, loud fart. The fake fart and surprised look on Zero's faced broke the tension in the room, and the hollow cave filled with a loud burst of laughter from everybody.

"OK, let's get back to business. Come on, Zero. Get over here and let's get this thing done." I waved Zero back over to the table and looked back down to the map, smoothing it out once again.

"What's Zero gonna do, Rock?" Howie asked me.

"One thing at a time, Howie. Right now, let's get back to this part of the plan." I bent back down to the map. "Slick and Jerry have quadrant one. Howie and Jim, you two have quadrant two. Is that clear?" The four guys looked at each other and nodded in agreement. "Quadrant three is the area north of Penrose Boulevard and west of Will Rogers." I outlined the boundaries with my finger. "That'll be Howard and Maloney's area, and quadrant four, over here, will be Blackburn's and mine. That's it for plan A. Any questions?"

"Yeah, Rock," Walt answered. "How'd you go about picking who would go with who? And what are your plans for Zero, Bobby, and me?" He pointed out the other guys with a questioning shrug of his shoulders.

"First, I picked Slick, Howie, and Gill as drivers because they each have cars that move. And Jerry, Jim, and Rick have rifles and know how to use them. As for me teamin' up with Bill? Well, he and I have a few extra things we've got to do while all you guys are taking care of Daddy Bruce, and I need his truck to haul the cans of gas."

"GAS? What the hell you gonna do with gas, Rock?" Walt and Rick asked simultaneously.

"It's all part of the second part of the plan. We're gonna burn down every one of those fuckin' wooden bridges!"

There was complete silence in the cave. Even Zero made no sound.

"Burn the bridges? Jesus Christ!" someone said.

"Cool! This is getting real cool. Burning the fucking bridges." Slick wandered out and around everybody else in a mesmerized stroll clapping his hands quietly together in front of him. "Shit, this will be a goddamn blast. Black out Brookshire and burn down the bridges."

Jerry was walking in a tight circle scanning all of the faces in the room, then he shot both arms straight up into the air toward the ceiling and shouted, "LET'S FUCKIN' DO IT!"

Everybody started hooting and hollering, jumping up and down until Bobby broke the excitement by shouting, "We could all go to jail for this, you know!"

Everyone grew quiet for a moment, then Jerry said, "You're damn right, we could, but we can't go to jail if we don't get caught and nobody squeals on us!"

More hooting and hollering followed. I raised my hands and shouted for everybody to cool it. "We've got to put together plan B, and both parts have to work perfectly or we *will* all go to jail. And, all of us have to swear complete allegiance and total secrecy to each other right now. Nobody, but nobody, squeals on any other member of the gang, and we stick together like glue. Nothing that happens or is talked about in Hucky Cove is ever to be talked about to anyone outside this cave or to anyone outside this gang. If anyone ever breaks these rules they'll be kicked out of the gang immediately, no questions asked. Agreed? Bill, pick up that big rock over there in the corner and bring it over here."

Bill placed the granite rock in the middle of the table after scooting the lantern and map over out of the way.

"OK. From now on this rock will represent our undivided unity and faith to the Pikes Peak High Gang. It will be our sacred stone. Let's each put one hand on this stone and pledge our allegiance and sworn secrecy to the gang. Come on, everybody, get a hand on it. One, two, three!"

All of us crowded around that little table with the granite rock sitting in the middle and placed our hands on top of it and on top of each other's hands. In scrambled unison, the pledge was given by everyone and the gang sealed itself into a single unit that no one would ever break.

Chapter *Thirteen*

After we completed our ritual around the rock, Zero headed out the cave's entrance saying he had to get some fresh air. Slick reached into his left shirt pocket and pulled out a pack of smokes. Tapping the pack against the palm of one hand, he selected one, put it to his lips, and lit it with his silver Zippo. The pungent odor of burning tobacco filled the cave almost instantly, then Slick turned to join Zero outside. The rest of us milled around settling in to the chairs and sofa.

From his corner of the couch, Bobby Hunt said, "How are we gonna coordinate the burning of the bridges with all of you guys shooting out the streetlights? Somehow we've got to know when you guys are off the hill so we don't strand you up there."

"I've got that all figured out," I said, "and as soon as Slick and Zero get back in here, I'll show you exactly how everything is gonna work. Bill, go get those two guys back in here. Tell 'em we're ready to start laying out plan B."

Bill headed out the cave entrance just as Zero came running back in, pushing Bill to one side and shouting at the top of his lungs, "We're screwed! They know all about us and they're coming to get us right now! I knew we'd get caught! Let's get the fuck outta here!"

Slick was right behind him in a hurry but nowhere nearly as panicked as Zero. "Zero! Cool it!" Slick hissed. "There's no reason to get your underwear in a twist, but a new ritzy-ditzy red T-Bird is coming up the road with two broads in it. Probably just a couple of gorgeous chicks looking for some action with a cave full of love-starved mountain men."

"It's all over, I tell ya—the jig is up! Everybody run for it!" Zero was jumping up and down, waving his arms like a maniac when Slick grabbed him by his shirt lapels and pushed him hard against the cave wall.

"Zero! Jesus, you're a pain in the butt. Just cool it and everything will be OK. Now get your ass back over there behind everybody, shut the hell up, and walk out casually like the rest of us."

I moved up to the front and was about to head out of the cave when Bill shouted from outside, "Hey, guys! Everything's cool. It's just Jeannie, and it looks like she's got Jennifer with her."

As we filed past Slick and Zero, Slick let go of Zero, shoving him to the rear, shaking his own head in disgust.

We were standing out front when Jeannie pulled the T-Bird up behind Bill's truck and parked it. The doors opened and both girls got out.

Walt leaned over to me and whispered, "I thought Hucky Cove was a secret place nobody but Bill knew about."

A few of the other guys were whispering under their breath the disappointment of having girls around. "Shit. Girls screw up everything," someone mumbled quietly. Both Bill and I gave behind-the-back gestures telling the others to cool it as we walked up to meet our girls.

"Hi, beautiful," Bill said, reaching down to grasp both Jeannie's hands.

I walked up to Jennifer and gave her a hug and a quick kiss. Her arms went around my waist as I bent down to whisper in her ear. Low wolf-whistles and a few Yogi Bear "hey-hey-hey"s came from the crowd behind us.

"Hey, Jen, I love you. You know that, but I told you this gang was for guys only. What in the heck are you and Jeannie doing coming up here?"

"She called me this morning and said she knew where the gang's headquarters were and wanted me to come up here with her. She told me that her dad wouldn't let her see Bill anymore, and she knew she could see him up here without getting in any more trouble. So, I just decided to come along. Besides, I wanted to see you too. I told her what you'd said about the gang being only for guys, but she made her mind up and was going with or without me."

I eased up on the hug and Jennifer dropped her hands down to my sides hooking her thumbs in my belt loops.

Low murmurs and a few fake coughs and throat clearings were coming from behind us. I turned my head around with an intended disgusted look on my face, then turned back to Jennifer, looking down into her eyes. The noises behind us stopped.

"Look, honey. You and Jeannie have to get outta here. We've got to keep working on our plans so we can get this thing going tonight. Everything is cool and I'll fill you in later."

"Can Jeannie and I help?" Before I could answer, she quickly added, with an innocent look on her face, "I really want to, and I know Jeannie wants to really bad."

Bill and Jeannie came around the back of the T-Bird. Bill had his arm over her shoulders, holding her close to his side. He leaned over to one side, looking past me to the guys clustered behind us, then shifted his eyes back to me. "We need to talk," he said, "in private."

He nodded for Jen and me to follow him over to a big Ponderosa pine a few feet off to the side of his truck. More slang phrases knocking the presence of girls floated from the guys behind us. Slick and Bobby broke away and walked over to where we were standing.

"Hey, you guys." Slick's voice held an easy roughness of authority. "The rest of the guys want to know what's up."

Bobby broke in, giving each of the girls an insincere smile. He dropped the smile when he said to Bill and me, "The rest of the guys are getting a little pissed because we all agreed there wouldn't be any girls in the gang. They want to know what the hell's going on."

"Give us a few minutes more, will ya fellas? Jeannie wanted to see Bill, and this was the only way she could without getting in trouble with her old man." I left Jennifer's side and took a few steps toward Slick and Bobby.

Jennifer moved up with me. "Yeah, just give them a break. Besides, Jeannie has some information that might help out if you'll just give her a chance."

"Shit!" was Slick's only response.

"Come on, Rock, get the girls outta here," Bobby said.

"OK. Everyone just go back inside and give us a few more minutes. We'll be right there." I patted Bobby on the shoulder with a slight nudge to turn him around. "Just a few minutes, OK?"

Bobby and Slick turned back to the entrance to the cave and herded the rest of the guys inside along with the mutterings of impatience.

Bill and I turned back and joined Jen and Jeannie by the big pine. "Jeannie's got some interesting information, and I think you ought to hear her out, Rock," Bill said. He moved up and put his arm around Jeannie's waist, and she did the same to him. I reached down to hold Jen's hand and we stood facing the other couple. "Go on, Jeannie, tell Rock what you told me."

"Well," she began, "I know you guys don't want us girls around—Jen told me that—but I think you should know some stuff that I can tell you about the streetlights and how the Brookshire Power Company repairs them.

"They have a system they follow, and if you do this right they'll never figure out what you're doing until it's too late. And I can get their work schedules and route priorities, which will show you when the work crews are short and other stuff like that. My dad has all that information in his office, and I know right where it is. Plus I can find out exactly where Daddy Bruce will be."

Jennifer quit talking and looked at me, then at Bill, waiting for one of us to say something. Bill looked at me. "Hmmm, that sounds pretty damn neat. Are you sure you can get this information?"

"Yep."

"We'll need it PDQ—within the next couple of hours. Can you get it that fast?" I asked her.

Jeannie dropped her arm from around Bill's waist and said, "Jen, will you go with me?"

"Sure. Sounds like fun to me. But won't your dad be a little suspicious if I go with you?"

"He's not usually at the hotel on Saturdays because he goes golfing with the uppity-ups, and his secretary is used to me bringing a buddy up to show them my dad's office." She looked back at Bill and me, "Whaddya think?"

"Sounds great to me." I looked over at Bill. "Give us just a few minutes to go talk it over with the rest of the fellas."

We walked back to the cave, and the girls went over to the rear of Bill's pickup, dropped the tailgate, and hopped up on it, dangling their legs.

After we explained the situation to the rest of the gang, the general reaction was suspicion. Walt was the first to speak. "If we let those two in, then we'll have to let everybody else's girl in later, and you know as well as I do that a bunch of girls will do nothin' but cause trouble." He looked around.

"Yeah," Slick jumped in, "if they want to help us with some information, maps or other stuff, fine. But we don't want them in the gang or at our meetings. If they'll agree to our terms, I don't mind if they help out. How about the rest of you guys?" Slick looked around at the others, then turned back to us. "Would they be willing to go along with us on those terms?"

Bill nodded yes. "All she and Jen want to do is help. Rock and I will keep our girls under control and make sure everything they do for us will be kept a secret. And we won't let them in on anything we do in secret here. If all of you agree—wait, we should take a vote."

Slick held up his right hand high in the air. "All those in favor of letting Jeannie and Jen work as outside spies for the Pikes Peak High Gang, raise your right hand."

Everybody raised their hand, except Zero.

"Now what the hell's your problem, Zero?" Slick said.

"I just don't want any girls in this outfit." He slumped his shoulders and turned toward the wall.

"Goddamnit, Zero! Are you gonna be anything else but a big pain in the ass? What the hell's your problem anyway? Quit acting like a goddamn baby, would ya!" Howie looked over at Zero and threw both hands up in the air in exasperation. "Screw Zero—we agree to let them work with us, but they can't come to our meetings or be an official part of the gang. That OK with the rest of you guys?"

Howie looked around the room. Bill and I waited for their reply. In murmured unison they all agreed—even Zero, although reluctantly.

"Bill and I'll go tell the girls." We turned and walked out of the cave.

Jennifer and Jeannie were still sitting on the tailgate. "Well?" they said in unison.

"You're in!" Bill said with a smile on his face.

The girls turned to each other and shook hands. "Great. What do you want us to do?"

Bill and I explained the rules to them and sent them down the mountain to get the information on the power company and Daddy Bruce. They promised they'd be back in a couple of hours with the scoop and hopped in Jeannie's T-Bird and drove off.

"Nice car," I said to Bill as we walked back into the cave.

"Yup. Her daddy bought it for her birthday."

Chapte *Fourteen*

Back inside the cave, I leaned over and smoothed out the map with both hands. The other guys all circled in.

"Does everybody understand the plan so far?" I asked, looking around the room.

"What's up with the girls?" Howie asked.

Bill stood up straight and motioned with his right hand that they would be back in a couple of hours with some information that would help us out in our final planning stages of the operation.

"We've got a lot of work to do before they get back up here, so let's get with it. Zero, this is where you, Walt, and Bobby come into the picture."

Zero pushed his way up to the table between Slick and Jerry. "I'm ready! What do you want me to do?"

Walt and Bobby wedged their way up to the other edge of the table to my right.

Leaning over the table with both my hands spread out on the map, I looked up at Walt and Bobby. "You two fellas, along with Zero, have the most important and the most dangerous job of the entire operation." I turned to look right into Zero's eyes, then stood up straight and pointed my finger in his face. "And, Zero, if you screw this up we'll all cook!"

"I *won't* screw up. I'll do whatever you want me to do. You guys can count on me." Zero pivoted back and forth shaking his tight fists up and down in front of him.

"OK, OK, let's settle down to business—and, Zero, pay close attention."

Chapter *Fifteen*

Jeannie pulled her T-Bird into a parking spot next to the empty space that had her dad's name painted on the stucco wall in front of it.

"Are you sure it'll be OK for me to go up there with you?" Jen asked.

"Come on, it'll be just fine. Besides, I'll need your help trying to find the maps and time schedules in Dad's files. Come on, let's go. We don't have a whole lotta time before Dad might show up."

Jeannie pulled the right side of the double-glass doors open and walked in while turning to wave Jen to follow her. Both girls rushed over to the elevator in the tiny lobby of the Brookshire office building, and Jeannie pushed the up button. The elevator doors slid open, and the girls walked into the cubicle. Jeannie turned around to the button panel as the doors closed behind them. She pushed the button for the fourth floor—"Executive Chambers" scrolled in bright gold letters next to the button. Quiet classical music filled the elevator as it quickly lifted them up to the executive floor. When the doors of the elevator opened, Jeannie immediately stepped out. Jennifer eased into the office receiving area slowly looking all around. She was surrounded in plushness like she'd never seen before and her feet seemed to sink into the thickest gold carpet she'd ever felt.

"Jen, this is Mrs. Clatworthy, my dad's secretary," Jeannie said.

Jennifer stiffened a bit, then calmly walked up to the front of the desk, which was situated in the back center of the room. Mrs. Clatworthy was standing behind her desk leaning over with her right hand extended out to shake Jen's. The woman appeared to be in her early thirties and wore a dark blue velvet dress with a dainty but brilliant gold aspen leaf pinned to the left side of her dress just below the shoulder. A string of pearls dropped down from her neck sweeping down just above the point where the first button of her dress was clasped. Tiny gold aspen earrings hung from each of her ear lobes and matched her broach.

"Nice to meet you, Jennifer. I always enjoy meeting Jeannie's friends." Jennifer placed her hand into Mrs. Clatworthy's and was surprised at how firmly the lady grasped her hand. It was more like a man would shake hands than a woman, she thought.

"What brings you and your friend up here, sweetheart? Your father's not in and I don't expect him in until a bit later."

"Oh, Jen and I were just bummin' around and I thought I'd show her Dad's office."

"Well, you girls just go right in, and there are some sodas and candy bars in the cabinet next to Mr. Fitzgerald's bookshelf. Help yourself."

"OK. Thanks, Mrs. Clatworthy. We won't be long."

Mrs. Clatworthy sat back down as Jeannie grabbed Jen's hand and led her down a hallway through two huge wooden doors. Both doors swung wide open when Jeannie pushed a button on the wall. Still holding Jen's hand, Jeannie led the way into her father's office.

"That's my dad's desk. The files we need to look in are behind those cabinet doors over there." Jeannie pointed to a wall that had cherry wood doors extending all the way from the floor to the ceiling.

Jen didn't even hear Jeannie's command. She walked up and behind the huge solid oak desk in the rear of the big room. The entire wall behind the desk was one humungous picture window. From where she was standing, she looked out over the entire rear of the

Brookshire complex. She could see the entire lake and all the buildings and everything else that surrounded it, plus the Rocky
Mountains rising up high behind the resort. It was the most spectacular sight Jennifer had ever seen.

"Jen. Jen. Jennifer!" Jeannie had to shout quietly to get Jen's attention.
"Come on, girl. We've got work to do."

"But, but, it's so beautiful." Jennifer turned to look back out the window.

"I know. Now come on over here and help me. We've got to get this
stuff and get it back up to the boys as fast as we can so they know they
can count on us."

Jen snapped out of her trance and moved quickly over to Jeannie,
who was leafing through a long file drawer.

"Jen, you go over to that file cabinet and look under 'Sheriff Bruce.'
Somewhere in there you should find his work schedule along with the
schedule of all of the other officers."

Jen darted over to the other file and opened the drawer labeled "B."
Flipping through the manila folders, she finally came to one with the
name "Bruce, Sheriff" on the tab.

"Found it!" She was just lifting it out of the drawer when Mrs.
Clatworthy's voiced filled the room.

"How are you girls doing in there, Jeannie?"

Jen let out a high-pitched scream and dropped the Bruce file onto the
floor, scattering papers in all directions.

"Shhh! *Keep quiet, Jen!*" Jeannie said as rapidly and forcefully as she
could without shouting. "It's only Mrs. Clatworthy on Dad's intercom."
Jeannie hurried over to her father's desk, leaned over toward a black box
on his desktop, and pushed a button. "We're doing just fine. We'll be out
in a minute."

"But I thought I heard one of you girls scream. Is everything all
right?"

Pressing the button on the box again, Jeannie replied, giggling, "Oh, I just snuck up behind Jennifer while she was looking out the window and scared her. She's OK, really."

Jeannie let up on the intercom button, and Mrs. Clatworthy said, "Well, OK, but you girls don't get into any trouble in there."

"We won't, and I'm sorry if we worried you, Mrs. Clatworthy. We'll be out in a minute. Thank you."

Jennifer was on her hands and knees collecting all the papers in the Bruce file. She was taking great care to make certain that they were replaced as orderly as possible.

"Is this what you're looking for, Jeannie?"

"That's it. Now put the file back and let's get outta here before Mrs. Clatworthy gets suspicious and comes in here."

"Did you get the map we were after?" Jen pointed toward a folded piece of paper in Jeannie's hand. Jeannie held it up in the air and nodded yes.

"Come on—let's go! No, wait a minute. Let's grab a pop and a candy bar from that cabinet over there so we can carry them out with us when we leave."

After they each got a bottle of pop and a Butterfinger, Jeannie grabbed Jen's hand and headed out through the big doors. Jeannie pushed another button on the wall and the doors slowly swung open, letting them out.

"Slip the papers inside your jacket so Mrs. Clatworthy won't see them," Jeannie whispered to Jen as she pushed the map inside her own jacket.

"Sorry I screamed, Mrs. Clatworthy, but Jeannie scared the daylights out of me! Sure didn't mean to upset you," Jennifer said, putting out her hand to shake Mrs. Clatworthy's again. "Good-bye! And thanks!"

Once they were outside the building, the girls ran to Jeannie's car and headed back up to the cave.

Chapter *Sixteen*

"We'll decide exactly how to plan the blackout process," I told the guys, "as soon as Jen and Jeannie get back with Daddy Bruce's schedule, the maps, and the work schedules of the power company's crew." I took a ball-point pen and circled each of the bridges showing their exact location at Seven Falls Road, Stover Road, Will Rogers Street, and Alsace Way.

"Those are the four main roads coming down off the Brookshire Hill," Slick said, "but what about the big bridge coming off Highway 85 onto Penrose Boulevard? All you've talked about are *four* bridges, but there are actually *five*. Aren't we gonna torch that big baby? Penrose is the main entrance to the hotel from Fort Carson coming from the south."

"Yup. You're right," I replied, "but don't worry about it. Remember I said Bill and I had something else we were gonna be responsible for? Well, the Penrose bridge is all ours. You guys take care of the other four bridges, and we'll torch the fifth one."

Walt stood up from the table taking a step back, "How in God's name are we gonna figure all of this out? How will we know when to torch the bridges? If we put a match to them too soon, all of you guys will be stranded on the other side."

"I know, Walt. That's why it's very important that we make sure all of us are synchronized and work together as one solid unit. Everybody go find a seat and Bill and I will go over the whole shebang."

As everyone sat on the couch, in a chair, or against the cave's wall, I walked slowly back and forth in front of them. Bill was standing behind me. Rubbing my hands and staring down at the floor as I paced the floor, I stopped, looked up at the rest of the gang, and pointed at them with both hands.

"This is how it will go down."

"Hey, Bill, Rock! We're back!" At the loud shout of Jeannie's voice everybody looked toward the entrance to the cave.

"Don't let 'em in here!" Zero jumped up from the couch, pointing at me with one hand and the entrance to the cave with the other.

As I walked toward the cave's entrance, Bill moved along behind me, and Slick pushed Zero back down into the couch. Zero started to bounce back up but thought better of it when Slick stared down at him and didn't move.

Both girls were standing together when the two boys emerged from the cave. When Jennifer saw me she rushed up, jumping up and down with nervous excitement right into my arms and almost instantly pushed herself away.

"Gawd! You wouldn't believe it! Just when I found the file on the sheriff in her father's filing cabinet, Jeannie's old man's secretary, Mrs. Clatworthy, said something over the speaker on his desk and I screamed and almost peed my pants!"

Jeannie was snuggled into Bill's side with his arm around her shoulders. She slapped Bill on his stomach, "Yeah. She almost screwed the whole thing up but we got everything you wanted." Jeannie handed Bill the utilities map and both girls broke out in laughter, "Gawd we were scared. If old lady Clatworthy would have caught us neither one of you guys would have ever heard from us again."

"Was your old man there?" Bill asked.

"Nope. He was off golfing or something. It was cool but he could have showed up at any time."

"When he finds this stuff missing from his files on Monday, the jinx will be up and we'll be two pieces of dead meat!"

"Jesus, Rock, I never thought of that. He'll sure as shit know we were the ones that stole it when he asks Clatworthy."

The two boys and Jennifer were walking in tight circles in a kind of stationary panic when Jeannie grabbed hold of Bill's hand motioning for the others to calm down with her free hand.

"Cool it, you guys. There's nothing to worry about. Jennifer apparently didn't notice, but there are plenty of copies of these things in the files. Dad keeps lots of spares around because a lot of his people need them for meetings and other business stuff. He'll never miss 'em."

"Fuckin—A. I thought we were screwed big time." I reached over and put my arm around Jennifer's waist pulling her in close while patting Bill on the shoulder. Bill leaned down and gave his girl a big kiss. I did the same.

"You gals did a super job. Thanks a bunch for all your help." I motioned back toward the cave, "The rest of the guys are probably getting a little up tight about what's taking so long so you two better beat it back down the mountain."

"Hold on a sec. The chicks can stay." Slim was leading the rest of the guys out from the cave's entrance, "We kind of had a little meeting of our own while you guys were out here. We figured that if you two were willing to put it on the line for the rest of us we should let you in the gang." He quickly added, "But we won't put up with any of your shit, OK!"

Bill and I had a look of complete disbelief on our faces. Jeannie and Jennifer looked at each other then back at the tight circle of boys and shouted in unison, "Really?"

"Yeah. Everything is cool with us isn't it fellas?" Slim looked back over his shoulder. There was a low grumbling rumble of approval.

"It's cool for now but it's just a test period and if you screw up you're both outta here!" Zero shouted throwing one of his arms up in the air. He was standing on his tip-toes in order to rise above the rest of the gang standing in front of him.

"You guys sure about this. The girls are OK with the way things are, aren't you?" Bill said looking at both of them.

The two girls slumped their shoulders and put on their best version of disappointed puppy-dog faces, "Yeah, we don't want to mess things up for you guys," Jeannie said while moving back toward Bill.

"Naw, it's OK. You guys are in." Slim turned and herded the rest of the gang back into the entrance to the cave.

Bill and I moved toward the cave to join the others and the two girls jumped up and down screaming as they hugged each other.

"Come on Jenny." I grabbed hold of her hand leading her into the cave. Bill put his arm around Jeannie and headed in, "We've got work to do."

Chapter *Seventeen*

When the girls entered the main room of the cave they were holding hands looking around. The light from the lanterns were bouncing huge silhouettes of distorted bodies all across the sides stretching up to the dome of the cave's roof.

Jennifer leaned over and whispered into Jeannie's ear, "This is really cool."

"Before we go any further we need to officially initiate the gals into the gang." Bobby had already bent over to pick up the swearing-in stone and placed it in the center of the card table. Bill and I motioned for the girls to come over to the table.

"Place your right hand on the rock and the rest of you guys circle around and put your right hands on top of theirs."

It took only a few minutes to gather the entire gang around the table. The sacred stone was completely engulfed by the hands and the oath of secrecy was given and accepted by both girls.

"OK, lets get down to business." I picked up the stone and handed it to Slick who walked over and placed it next to the cave's wall to his left. Bill handed the map to me, which was removed from the table so the swearing of the girls could take place without damaging the map. Once again he spread the map out across the table.

"Before I go any further does anyone have a question about how the quadrants are laid out and who is designated to which quadrant?"

"I still want to know where I fit in." Zero said.

"We'll get to that in a minute. Walt and Bobby are just as curious as you are, Zero. Just be patient."

Nobody else said a thing. I picked up the map and folded it putting it on the chair directly behind me, then gestured to Bill to hand me the utility service route map the girls stole from Jeannie's dad's office. I unfolded and spread it over the table.

"Fantastic!" I said as the map spread out over the tiny table top. "I didn't know anything like this even existed. It shows every streetlight's location and in what order of priority they're repaired in relation to the maintenance repair panel back at the utility headquarters building. When a specific streetlight goes out it apparently shows up on an electrically coordinated grid board back at the repair office terminal. When a streetlight goes out they know exactly where to send a repair truck out to fix it. With a little planning we will be able to get those repair crews running around in circles and they won't catch on to what's happening until it'll be too late. Jeannie, this is really cool! OK fellas come up here and crowd around the table."

Jeannie and Jennifer moved in behind me and Bill. The rest of the gang moved up next to the tiny table looking down at the map.

I kind of swept my hand over the entire map, looking up and around into all of the curious eyes looking down over the new map.

"Don't let all of the dots and colored lines scattered all across this map's surface confuse you. If you'll notice, the basic layout of this map is exactly the same as the other map I drew the four quadrants on before."

I traced with my index finger the two dissecting roads that divided the Brookshire community into four equal segments. Moving my finger the entire length of Penrose Boulevard, showing the west to east boundary, then going vertically from north to south along Will Rogers Road, splitting Brookshire down the middle in the other direction.

"If you look at this map closely you'll see that the farthest streetlight on the grid from the utility maintenance building is in Howie and Jim's quadrant, number two. You two guys will be the first ones to shoot out a streetlight, this one right here. It is at the corner of Swan and Long's Peak Road."

Howie broke in. "When will we know what time we should snuff that light?"

"Yeah, and what do we do after we nail it?" Jim's question turned everybody's attention to him then shifted back toward me.

"We'll get to the timing of all of this later. Right now I want to lay out the plan of attack. If we're gonna get this in operation for tonight we've got to get busy so all of you need to…"

"Wait a minute! Wait a minute." Bill and I turned around and everybody stood up and looked at Jeannie.

"What, now?" Zero said, throwing both of his arms into the air running back away from the table, "See? I told you the bitches would be trouble. Haven't done a damn thing yet and they're already…"

"Goddamn it! Shut up, you stupid son-of-a-bitch!" Bill shouted, pointing his finger across the table directly at Zero. "I've about had it with your stupid ass—get the hell out of here!" He moved quickly around the table toward Zero, pushing his way through the crowd of boys. He moved up to Zero and pushed him hard, making him stumble almost falling before he regained his balance.

"Hey, you cock-sucker, leave me alone!"

Bill pushed him again, and Zero swung his right fist, hitting Bill hard in the left shoulder. In a split second Bill lunged at Zero, grabbing him by the shirt with his left hand and hitting him hard, square in the nose with his right fist. Zero was swinging like a wild man, hitting Bill at random but not landing a punch anywhere that hurt Bill.

Before anyone realized what was happening, Bill and Zero were pushing and fighting their way out the cave's entrance.

By the time the rest of the gang organized itself enough to rush out of the cave, Bill was already sitting on top of Zero, who was blindly flailing up at Bill with both arms. Bill was trying to catch Zero's arms, and eventually he had both of them pinned down on the ground and was moving up alongside of Zero's body, placing both of his knees on Zero's arms and pinning them to the ground. Zero was helpless, trying to twist and turn his body violently in a futile attempt to get out from under the cowboy's control. Bill slapped the shouting boy hard across the face and then grabbed both of his shirt lapels in two tight fists, lifting Zero's head off the ground while still pinning his arms down on the ground with his knees. Zero gave out a pain-filled groan.

"Now, you little smart-ass son-of-a-bitch, listen and listen good or I'll beat the livin' shit out of ya right here!" His face was beat red and a fraction of an inch away from Zero's.

"If you so much as fart loud enough so I can hear it, I'll pound your ass right into the ground. I've had it with your whining, ugly ass. Do you read me?" Bill shook him hard. "Do you read me, you little bastard? Shut your ass up, and if you so much as look in Jeannie's or Jen's direction you won't see the other side of next Sunday. Now, shut the fuck up!"

He was shaking Zero so hard his neck lost all of its tension and his head snapped up and down like a rag doll with the back of his head banging hard against the graveled ground with each thrust downward.

"OK, OK! I give! I give!"

"Promise me, you little bastard!"

"OK, I promise! I promise!"

With Zero's screaming acceptance Bill pushed him hard one more time and stood up directly over the beaten boy, who was close to crying. The cowboy pointed his finger straight down at Zero and backed off, not saying another word. Walking away, he went over and leaned against the side of his pickup with his head bent down looking into the empty bed of the truck. Jeannie ran over to him putting her arm around his waist.

The rest of the boys moved slowly back into the cave except for Jennifer and me. Zero was sitting up wiping the blood that was dripping down his upper lip from his nose with his shirtsleeve. I moved around in front of Zero, and looking him right in the eye, said, "You either shape your ass up right now or get the hell out of here, ya hear?"

Looking up at me he nodded, putting his hands behind him pushing himself up. Standing with his shoulders slumped he looked at me, then down to the ground. In a whisper he said, "Yeah, I hear." He turned and wobbled his way back into the mouth of the cave.

Jennifer stood outside the cave's entrance as I went over to Bill and Jeannie.

"Come on, you guys. It's over. Let's get back inside and put this thing together. I don't think we'll have anymore trouble with Mr. Z." I put my hand on his shoulder, and we turned back toward the cave.

"If he says anything else about Jeannie, I'll kill the little bastard, Rock."

"I know, but I don't think he'll give us any more trouble."

Chapter *Eighteen*

When the four of us entered the big cavern, Zero was sitting in isolation over in a far corner of the room. He didn't look at us or the girls; instead he just sat slumped over in his chair pouting like a little boy. The rest of the gang was scattered around the room, filling all of the remaining chairs and sofa with a couple of boys leaning up against the wall of the cave. I moved to the center of the room, glancing over in Zero's direction. "The way Zero kept bitching and moaning every time some little thing went a little wacky, it was bound to happen that something or somebody was eventually gonna crack," I said.

"Yeah, but..." Zero protested.

"Shut up, Zero." Slick looked over at Zero, and the boy slumped back into his chair.

I moved forward just a bit, holding the palms of my hands out in front of me with a calming, downward motion. "Cool it, you guys. Everybody just cool it a minute. We've all got to agree to let this thing drop right now and get on with our main objective or dissolve the gang right here and now."

I paused for a moment, then stuck both hands in my back pockets.

"All of those in favor of keeping the Pikes Peak Gang together signify by raising their right hand."

I raised my hand first, Bill followed right after, and slowly everybody else raised their hands—including Zero, though reluctantly—except Slick, who stepped forward to the center of the room next to me. The girls looked at each other and refrained from participating, moving back toward the cave's entrance.

"Rock, I think we need to settle the problem with Zero before we go any further. We should take a vote as to whether he gets to stay in the gang or not. I think all of the guys agree. Don't you?"

The rest of the boys nodded their heads in silent agreement.

"OK, then,' I said. "Zero, I'm gonna ask you to leave while we take a vote. Go on outside and I'll send someone out to get you after we vote."

Zero got up from his chair and plodded his way through the loose crowd of boys and left the cave. After he was gone the room remained completely silent except for the constant shuffling of feet on the granite floor.

"Come on, let's get this over with. All those in favor of Zero staying in the Pikes Peak Gang raise your right hand."

"Just a minute," Bill said, stepping forward. "I won't apologize for beating the piss out of that sucker, but I would like to ask everybody to vote to keep him in the gang. I'll grant you he's a big pain in the butt, but I think he's an OK guy. And we'll need him.

"First, though, I think we should set down some rules everyone has to follow or they're out, no questions asked."

Once again, heads all over the room nodded in agreement.

"Let's vote, then. All of those in favor of Zero staying in the gang raise your right hand."

Everybody stuck their hands in the air. "OK, that's settled. He's in. Go out and bring him back in, Bobby," I said.

Zero reentered the room in front of Bobby with a big smile on his face. "I'm sorry, Bill," he said. "I won't be any more trouble, you guys, promise."

After a few minutes of discussion the gang set down a limited set of rules that were adopted by everyone. I moved back behind the table and motioned for Jeannie to come forward to tell the gang what she was going to say before the fight broke out.

"Jeannie has something she wants to say to us, and we need to listen to her. Go ahead, girl." I stepped back giving the floor to Jeannie.

"I just think you should wait until next weekend to make your move," she said quietly.

A bunch of murmurs and loud moans rumbled throughout the cavern "Wait a minute—let the girl finish," Zero said in a loud voice.

"Thanks, Zero. The reason I'm telling you to wait until next Saturday is that last night at dinner I overheard my dad telling my mom that Sheriff Bruce was going to be shorthanded and that one of the crews for the utility company was taking the weekend off."

"Cool! We'll have the run of the place!" someone shouted.

"Yeah," Slick agreed, "but what did he mean by Daddy Bruce being shorthanded?"

"Well, instead of the sheriff having three deputies on duty," Jeannie explained, "he'll only have one. Some guy named Deputy Delbert."

The room erupted with laughter. "Old da Delbert!"

"What are you guys laughing at? Dad said he's a nice guy."

"Yeah. Nice all right," Walt said with a chuckle.

"But not too bright," added Bobby.

"With Delbert as Bruce's sidekick they'll never catch us!"

I walked over and stood next to Bill. "This will be a slam-dunk," he said. "But let's get back to work. Everybody come up here and gather around the table and let's work this thing out." He reached over and patted Jeannie on the back. "Thanks, girl—that was great news."

Everybody moved up around the little table. Walt went over and picked one of the gas lanterns from where it was hanging on the wall and held it over the table. The orange light from the lantern reflected off the faces looking down at the map. An air of unifying solitude fell over the room. The Pikes Peak Gang was finally united into a solid unit, ready to undertake its first mission, Operation Blackout Brookshire. My voice became serious, and all the eyes and ears were tuned into my every word and motion.

"Howie, Jim, you two will make the first move." I pointed to the dot representing the streetlight at Swan and Long's Peak Road. "Jim will be the shooter, and Howie, you need to drive up close enough to the light so Jim can hit it but not so close that your car will be directly in the light.

"Immediately after you knock it out, drive around the corner where you can't be seen by the repair crew when they arrive."

"How do we know they'll come?" Howie asked.

"As soon as Jim shoots it out, it'll show up on the troubleshooting grid back at the utility headquarters, and they'll dispatch a crew out right away. It'll probably take them five or ten minutes to get there.

"When they finally do arrive, you guys go directly to the phone booth out in front of Sully's gas station, which is two blocks north of you on the corner of Blake and Pine."

"And then what?" Jim asked impatiently.

"Except for Zero, Walt, Bobby, Jeannie, Jennifer, and the rest of us will be parked over at the Brookshire horse stables, and I'll be stationed in front of the phone booth over there. Between now and then I'll copy the phone number down from the booth and get it to you guys. You'll call that number from the phone at Sully's, and I'll be at the stables to answer your call. The minute we hear from you, we'll head out to our designated quadrants and start blasting out every streetlight on the Brookshire Hill.

"After the utility repair team fixes the light at Swan and Long's Peak, give them ten minutes to get back to their office, then start shooting out every streetlight in your path. When the utility crew gets back to their office, there'll be at least half a dozen other lights out spread all over their troubleshooting grid. They'll get a new assignment and head out to fix the other lights.

"The only danger we'll have to face at that time is that we won't know for sure which light or quadrant they'll head to next. All of us will have to keep a sharp eye out for their truck. Whoever spots it first will have to work in those blocks outside of their view. If you have time you might want to swing back past the light that was repaired and blast it out again. You shouldn't have to worry too much about them being suspicious because they won't have caught on to what's happening yet. Just be sure to check for their truck before you blast each light. And nobody takes out a light if there is another car or anyone around who might see you."

I paused for a moment to see if there were any questions. Everyone was tuned in to me and nodding as though they understood. I continued, looking back down at the map. "If all of you look real hard at this map, you'll see that each one of these spots—the intersections of these streets where there's a streetlight—has a coded number next to it. You'll also see that they're numbered in consecutive order, starting with 289, which is the light located over here in Howie and Jim's quadrant at Swan and Long's Peak Road. The light at the furthest location from the utility headquarters is designated by the largest coded number for that quadrant. For instance, the light on the corner of Helen Hunt and Seven Falls Road is coded 160 and actually lights up the corner by the bridge where Zero will be stationed. In the extreme northeastern corner of Gill and Rick's quadrant, number three, at the corner of Schaffer and St. Clair, the code number is 81.

"Now," I said, about to wrap up the plan, "you'll notice there are lights near each of the bridges. These will be the very last lights we shoot out before we make our escape."

Looking over at Zero, Walt, Bobby, and the two girls, I pointed at each one of them and emphasized the importance of their staying hidden underneath each of their respective bridges.

"What will we be doing while all of you guys are shooting the lights out?" Walt asked.

"Yeah, we'll be missing out on all of the fun!" Bobby said, looking over in Walt's direction.

"If you guys will just wait a minute," Bill said, "Rock will get to your part in all of this. And believe me, you won't complain about missing out on all of the action." Bill was standing behind me with a cocky smile on his face. "You'll be putting the cherry on top of the chocolate sundae." He swung his arm in a short circle pointing his finger back to me. "Keep going, Rock."

I leaned back down to the map. "Howie, when you see the repair truck leave after fixing the light at Swan and Long's Peak, you and Jim move right back in and shoot it out again. Then start moving across your quadrant in an east-to-west pattern, zigzagging your way over to Will Rogers and back west to the far edge of the quadrant until you reach Circle Drive, which completely encircles the hotel resort and meets back up with Penrose Boulevard. There'll be two lights you won't have to worry about: the one up here by the Buffalo Park and the one over here where the little bridge goes over the road, connecting the two portions of the golf course on either side of Circle Drive. The light at the Buffalo Park is too far out of the way, and the one by the golf course is too close to the hotel and too risky—don't chance it.

"As soon as you hit the rest of the lights along the south side of Penrose Boulevard and this stretch of Circle Drive, you should have knocked out all of the lights in your quadrant. Head directly over to Seven Falls Road and get across the bridge as quickly as possible."

Looking over at Slick and Jerry, I diagrammed their course of attack, which started their shooting rampage on the north side of Penrose Boulevard from Will Rogers Road west along that section of Circle Drive that wrapped around to the south and west to Buffalo Park. From there they would follow the same basic zigzag pattern, west to east across quadrant one, until they ended up at the last streetlight, which lit up the bridge on Stover Road where they would meet up with Walt.

"Gill, you and Rick will blanket this quadrant, number three, working it from the corner of Will Rogers and Penrose Boulevard, and you'll move east, then back west until you end up at the Alsace bridge, where you'll rendezvous with Jeannie and Jen.

"While all of you guys are doing your jobs in these three quadrants, Bill and I will be knocking the hell out of every light in quadrant four. We'll work our way out to the Penrose Boulevard bridge, torch it, and then get the hell out of there."

"What about me?" Bobby said, standing up and looking around with a confused look on his face. "Nobody's picked me up at the Rogers bridge."

"You're right, Bobby. That means that you, Slick, and Jerry have to help Zero burn the Falls bridge, then the three of you will have to haul ass down to help Bobby torch the Rogers bridge." I looked up at the four boys and then said pointedly to Bobby, "Don't touch a match to the Rogers bridge until Slick and the other two guys get there." I turned to the others and said, "As soon as you guys get to Bobby, soak the bridge with gasoline and set it off. Then get the hell outta there!"

"How are we gonna get the gas?" Zero asked.

"Good question. Bill and I are gonna drive around to each bridge, next Saturday afternoon and put one five-gallon can of gas under each bridge. You won't have any trouble finding the can under your bridge because they'll be those big red ones.

"When the time comes to douse the bridge, make sure you soak the wooden supports under each side, and do it carefully, making sure that you don't splash any of that shit on yourselves. We don't want any of you guys going up in flames—just the bridges."

A round of nervous laughter filled the cave. Bill looked over to the girls. "And you gals wear jeans." The girls nodded.

I continued. "Right next to the gas cans, Bill and I will also leave a stick with some cloth wrapped around one end of it. After you soak the bridge supports with gas, sprinkle some on the rag, then back off as far as you can before you light the cloth torch. Make sure no cars are approaching the bridge before you light the torch. As soon as you light the torch, throw it under the bridge and move your butt out of there. When the torch hits the gas, it's gonna explode into one hell of a burst of flame. Don't stand around and watch—get out of there PDQ."

"What do we do if we see someone coming?" Jerry asked.

"Just wait until they go across the bridge and out of sight."

"Hell, it'll be Saturday night and busier than all get-out."

"No, it won't. We won't even start shooting out the lights until ten, and I figure it'll take each team about an hour and a half to shoot out each light in their quadrant. We'll be torching the bridges between eleven-thirty and twelve, and there should be hardly any traffic by that time."

I leaned back and looked around at the gang with a big smile on my face. I then reached over to Bill with my right hand, and the two of us shook hands. "It'll work. Goddamn it, it'll work!" We raised our fists high over our heads. "Operation Blackout Brookshire! The Pikes Peak Gang fights back!"

The musty cave erupted in shouts of excitement and unity. After a few minutes of rowdiness Bill raised his hand to calm us all back down.

"When Rock and I torch the Penrose bridge, we'll cut out of there and meet all of you guys back at the Pard. When all of us get there, we'll act as if nothing at all unusual has happened—just act like your normal selves. We won't celebrate until one o'clock next Sunday, when we'll all meet up here at the cave."

Jennifer asked if she could say something. The gang nodded their approval. "Just so nobody suspects us," she said, "maybe we should all go down to the Chief Theater and buy tickets for the nine o'clock show.

That way we can prove we weren't anywhere near Brookshire when all this broke out." She looked around and stepped back behind me.

"That's a super idea, Jen," Walt said. "If anyone asks us where we were Saturday night, we'll have proof we weren't anywhere around the hill." He moved over and gave Jen a high-five.

Just as everyone started to move out of the cave I shouted, "We'll all meet down at the Pard next Saturday, at noon. See you all there!"

Chapter *Nineteen*

It was one of those crisp November days, famous in Colorado, when deep blue Western skies engulf the snow-capped peaks of the Rockies and make them glow a brilliant white. I pulled Old Ironsides up to the curb in front of Jennifer's house. A few bright, white, fluffy clouds were trying to sneak around the edges of Pikes Peak. They didn't threaten bad weather, but just gave the peak a beautiful postcard look.

I got out of the car and started to walk up to the front door of the house when Jen came out. Her mother was right behind her, leaning out of the doorway and holding the storm door open with her left hand. "Hi, Ralph. Now you kids be careful and get Jennifer back by five."

I waved and gave her a thumbs-up. "Sure will, Mrs. Lucas! Thanks, and have a great day." Jen ran up to me and grabbed my left hand, turning me back toward Ironsides.

I opened the driver's side door, and Jennifer tucked her skirt under her as she scooted over to the middle of the front seat. I slid into the car right next to her and started the car, slipping it into gear and driving slowly away from the curb. Jennifer put her left arm up behind my head and was softly scratching the nap of my neck.

"Man, am I nervous about tonight. I don't think I've ever intentionally lied to my parents, and when I said you were taking me to the Chief tonight, they sure seemed to give me a funny look."

"Yeah, I know what you mean about being nervous, but everything will be cool. Don't worry about it. Besides, I just told my folks that I was going out with you tonight and that I'd be home a little after midnight."

"Darn! I didn't tell mom and dad that we were gonna be out after midnight. Jeez, I hope they'll let me stay out that late." She brought her arm down and leaned away, looking at me with a very serious expression on her face. "What'll I say to them at dinner?"

"Hmmm. I've got it: Tell them there's a double feature and you'll be home about one o'clock. You can also tell them we'll be double-dating with Blackburn and Jeannie. Your dad knows Jeannie's old man pretty well, and he'll talk your mom into letting you go." I put my arm up over Jennifer's shoulders and snugged her into my side. "It'll be cool. Don't sweat it." Keeping my eyes fixed on the road, I turned my head slightly to one side and bent down to give Jennifer a quick kiss on her lips. "We've got to hustle over to the Pard. We're running late."

I pulled into the drive-through lane and stopped next to the first speaker. Rolling down the window, I leaned out to be greeted by Mrs. Harding's voice welcoming us to their drive-in. "Just fine, Mrs. Harding. We'd like two cheeseburgers with curly fries and two medium cherry Cokes."

Mrs. Harding acknowledged our order and asked us to please pull forward.

Just as I passed the two sacks of burgers and fries over to Jennifer and got my change, thanking Mrs. Harding, I noticed the rest of the Pikes Peak Gang pulling their cars in behind us into the order lane. I looked into the rearview mirror and held my hand up so Walt could see it through the rear window, then pointed over to the corner of the parking lot where Bill had just pulled his truck up and parked. I could see Walt nodding that he got the message, in the mirror.

I drove across the lot and parked right alongside Bill's truck. He got out and walked around the back of the truck and up to my window, which was still rolled down.

"How're you two love birds doin'?"

"Fine, but we might have a bit of a problem tonight."

"What's up?"

"Well, Jen forgot to ask her folks if she could stay out until one, so we decided that she would tell them that we're going to a double feature at the Chief and that we would be double-dating with you and Jeannie. That OK with you?" I stuffed a half-dozen fries into my mouth and sucked up some soda through a straw.

"Shit! You can't tell 'em that! You know Jeannie isn't supposed to go out with me anymore! You'll get her ass in big-time trouble if Old Man Fitzgerald ever found out!"

"Damn, that's right! I completely forgot."

Jennifer put her burger down and turned to me in alarm. "What'll we do, Rock?"

I thought for a minute, swallowing my fries, then said, "OK, let's not panic. Let's just say we're going out with Bill and his girl and that we're gonna meet some of the other guys and their girls at the movie." I turned my head back and forth between the two of them, waiting for an answer. "That'll work, won't it?"

"Yeah, I suppose," Jen replied thoughtfully. "And if they ask me who Bill is dating, I'll just say I don't know for sure after Mr. Fitzgerald decided not to let his daughter date Bill anymore. Besides, my dad doesn't think Jeannie's dad is treating her right. In fact," she giggled, "he feels sorry for the both of you, Bill. I even think that if he knew you guys were sneaking out to see each other, he'd think it was cool."

"What'd you think, Bill?" I asked.

Jennifer and I both looked at him, waiting for his approval of the new plan.

"I suppose that it would be cool. Yeah, let's do it that way." He then looked right past me to Jennifer and pointed his finger at her. "Just don't bring up Jeannie. I don't want her old man to get a drift of what we're doin'."

Jennifer shook her head in agreement and resumed eating. Bill moved up and away from the window as the rest of the gang huddled in between the truck and Ironsides.

"What's happenin'?" Walt leaned over to look in the window. The other boys just milled around talking amongst themselves. I took another bite of my burger, then put it back inside the paper bag and took a handful of fries and handed the bag over to Jennifer. Walt moved away from the car's door, and I stepped out, moving to the side and shutting the door behind me. Bill had moved through the crowd of boys to the back of his truck where he motioned for me to come over for a look. He pointed down to a row of red army-issue five-gallon gas cans. Each can had a heavy, metal screw cap on top attached by a long, heavy metal-link chain. Bill played with one of the chains on top of the closest can. It rattled against the metal as he flicked it back and forth with his finger.

"I got these out of the attic of our old hay barn and filled each one of them with gas from our bulk gas tanks. I don't think my dad will even notice the gas is missing because the gauge needle on the tank didn't even move. But I'm gonna have to get them back immediately after we're done with them before dad notices that they're gone."

"You mean you already filled them up?" I asked, incredulous.

"Yup, plum full. What do we do now?"

"Well, let's take off and put one can under each bridge," I said. "I did change my mind a little bit, though. I don't think you and I should do it all because it would take too long. So let's give one can to each of the teams and let them put it under their assigned bridge. You take the one that you and I will be using and put it under the Penrose bridge, and Jen and I will take two cans and put one each under the Alsace bridge, where she and Jeannie will be, and we'll also take the can to the Rogers bridge where Bobby will be. Hey, Slick, Jerry—come on over here."

The two boys moved over to the side of the truck. "You two guys get Walt," I said, "and take this can of gas and head over to the Stover bridge and put it underneath there. Make sure you hide it so it's completely out of sight.

"Howie, Jim! Hey Zero! You guys take this one and head over to the Falls bridge and do the same thing. Now, make sure you guys hide that sucker real good."

The two trios of boys took their respective gas cans out of the back of the truck and placed them in the trunks of their cars. I hefted out one can and put it on the ground, then lifted out another one and carried them both over to the rear end of Ironsides and lifted one heavy can at a time into the trunk, standing them upright against the spare tire. I propped the pile of snow chains that were lying in a heap at the far back of the trunk up against the second can of gas so they wouldn't fall over and shut the trunk with a heavy thud. I turned around and waved for the rest of the gang to come and gather around me.

"Now, when you get to your bridge," I told them, "don't be in a big hurry. Make sure there aren't any other cars coming when you carry the gas can down to hide it under the bridge. Make sure nobody sees you do it! And as soon as you're done, get the hell out of there. Let's go, and everybody meet right here at eight o'clock tonight. And don't forget to go to the Chief and buy your tickets for tonight's show. Make sure to tear the ticket in half and keep only one half of the stub—and don't lose it. Without those ticket stubs, we're cooked if somebody asks us where we've been tonight and we can't produce the tickets as proof. If there aren't any questions, let's get moving!"

Everybody climbed into their cars and headed out of the parking lot with Jennifer and me trailing the pack.

"Jesus Christ! We're really gonna do this, aren't we!" Jennifer wasn't really talking to me; she just mumbled the words out loud to herself as she took another bite of her cheeseburger.

"Fuckin' A!" I gave her a cocky smile, and she playfully slugged me on the shoulder for using the 'F' word in front of her. Then she looked right at me and said, "Fuckin' A!" and we both laughed out loud.

I turned Old Ironsides out of the parking lot and headed up over the top of the Eighth Street hill toward one of the five wooden bridges that would be turned into a pile of charred ashes within the next twelve or so hours. The first step of Operation Blackout Brookshire was underway, and the beginning of the legend of the Pikes Peak Gang was about to begin.

Chapter *Twenty*

Turning right on to Cheyenne Road, I made certain to keep to the thirty-five-mile-per-hour speed limit. After what seemed like the longest mile I'd ever driven in my life, I came to the four-way intersection of Cheyenne and Will Rogers Roads. I turned on the left turning signal and waited for the blue '61 Ford on my right to move through the intersection and head up the hill toward the Brookshire Hotel. After the Ford pulled away, I made the left turn and moved across the intersection and pulled Ironsides across the street onto a small gravel-covered parking area just twenty-five feet or so on the north and west side of the Will Rogers bridge. Putting the car in park, I left the engine idling. Both of us turned and looked each other in the eye.

"Here goes…"

Jen didn't say a word, but I could see the frightened look in her eyes. I reached down to the door handle with my left hand, opened the door, and stepped out of the car, turning to walk back toward the trunk. I left the door open and stepped a couple of steps away before turning back. Stooping over and placing my left hand on the front seat, I leaned into the car and reached around the steering column and turned the keys to shut off the engine, then removed them. "Can't open the trunk without these."

That broke the tension between the two of us, and Jen quickly snapped her left hand across my arm and said in a muffled shout, "God, would you hurry up? I'm so nervous I'm about to wet my pants!"

I gave her a quick smile and backed out of the car, heading back to the trunk. I inserted the key into the lock on the trunk and the lid popped open. Before I reached in for the gas can I looked back over my left shoulder and checked the intersection for any cars or people walking along the roadside. The coast was clear behind me, but when I bent over to peek around the edge of the raised trunk, a blue Chevy pickup truck was coming down the hill. The truck was slowing down much sooner than it needed to before reaching the stop sign at the intersection. My mind was spinning ninety miles an hour. "Shit! He's gonna stop! What'll I do? What'll I say?" I could feel little beads of sweat rolling down my sides from my armpits. I slowly raised up from looking in the trunk, reaching my right arm up and over the top of the trunk's lid as if I were about to close it. As calmly as I could, I turned my head to look over at the truck, which was pulling over to the other shoulder of the road. And whoever it was, was rolling down his window.

"Hello, Rock!"

It was Mr. Bamford, the chemistry teacher.

"You and…" He stuck his head partially out the window and bent his head back just a bit so he could see Jen in the front seat of Ironsides. "Oh," he said, "it's you, Jennifer." He waved to her.

I couldn't see past the trunk lid to see her reaction, but she must have made the right moves because Mr. Bamford turned back to look at me. He was moving about in the cab of his truck like he was going to get out.

"You kids OK? Need any help?"

I saw that he was going to get out so I quickly slammed the trunk lid down, looked both ways up and down the street, and sprinted across the road over to his truck. I was making motions with my arms, waving him off to indicate that everything was just fine, and hoping to keep my teacher from getting out of his truck.

"Naw, we're doing A-OK. Everything's cool, Mr. Bamford."

By this time I had made it across the street and was leaning into the truck with my arms on the edge of his window. With a big smile on my face I told him, as calmly as I could, "Jennifer and I just thought it was such a nice day we were going to have a little walk along the creek."

Mr. Bamford gave me a sly wink with his right eye and looked over my shoulder at Jen in the car across the street. Not looking directly at me, he nodded toward her and called out, "You have a good time, Jennifer, and keep a sharp eye on this young fella." Turning back to me, he said, "You kids have fun now—and be careful."

I leaned back away from the truck as he pulled away. After a slow pause, he pulled away and headed east. He had his left arm raised out his window, waving good-bye to us.

"Hang tight, Jen. The coast is clear, and I'm hauling that can down under the bridge as fast as I can!"

I popped the trunk open, reached in, and grabbed the heavy gas can out of the trunk with a grunt. Staggering from the lopsided weight of the can, I shuffled over to the creek bank on the west side of the bridge and moved ever so slowly down the steep embankment to the very edge of Cheyenne Creek. Once I regained level footing again along the narrow footpath paralleling the tiny stream's side, I moved in toward the shadow of the wooden bridge overhead. About midway under the bridge I hefted the gas can up closer to the base of the huge wooded beam along the underside of the bridge. Wiggling it back and forth I snugged the can up against the beam. It wasn't going anywhere until Bobby came later that night. I turned to head out from under the bridge. Before I left the shadow of the bridge I heard the bridge rattle above me and felt the ground under my feet shake a little from the weight of a car or truck moving quickly over my head.

As soon as I got out from under the bridge, I scrambled up the bank and moved quickly up the bank and back into my car. The car that had driven over the bridge just a few seconds before was pulling away from the stop sign onto the eastbound lane of Cheyenne Road.

Inside the car, Jennifer had her head bent down, holding her face in both of her hands. With my arm around Jen, I pulled back out onto Will Rogers Road, squeezing her tightly into my side. Jen took her face away from her hands and looked straight ahead.

"I thought we were dead meat! I don't think I've ever been that scared before in my whole life! When Bamford stopped I thought for sure we..."

Jen just kept babbling on and on for the next two blocks or so, and then we both broke out into hysterical laughter. I was laughing so hard I had to pull over to the side of the road and stop the car.

After a few minutes we settled down and headed toward Alsace Way to put the other gas can under that bridge.

"God, Rock! Can you *believe* how close we were to getting caught by Bamford? If he'd gotten out of his truck and come over, I don't know *what* I would've done!" She leaned hard into my side. "Let's get over to the Alsace bridge and get rid of that other can and get out of here."

"As soon as we hide that one," I agreed, "let's head downtown to the Chief and get our tickets." I hugged her even closer.

We pulled up to one end of the Alsace bridge. I grabbed the last can of gas out of the trunk and hauled it down and under the bridge, putting it in a spot that would be out of sight. There wasn't any traffic this time, and when I was finished we drove over to Nevada Avenue and headed into town to the theater.

"This is gonna be a great night!" I said as I glanced over at Jen. She looked up and I gave her a quick kiss.

Chapter *Twenty-One*

When Jen and I pulled in to the parking lot behind the Chief Theater, Bill and Jeannie were just coming around the back corner of the building, heading toward Bill's truck. I pulled Ironsides into a marked parking spot a couple of spaces down from Bill's truck. Jen and I got out and walked around the other parked cars over to meet Bill and Jeannie. Jen dropped my hand, which she was holding, and ran over to her friend. Waving her arms up and down and jumping toward Jeannie, she stopped and pointed back toward me. "Jeez," she squealed, "you guys wouldn't *believe* how close we came to getting caught by old man Bamford!"

"Bamford?" Jeannie said, glancing first at me, then at her boyfriend.

Jennifer told them the whole story. When she finished they moved over to the rear of the pickup. Bill dropped the tailgate and the two girls hopped up and sat down on it, dangling their legs over the edge. Bill put his right foot on the bumper next to Jeannie and leaned on the side of his truck. I did the same thing on the other side.

"We didn't have a lick of trouble over at the Penrose bridge. That street is always busy this time of the day, and I just waited for a little break in the traffic and hauled the can right down the bank and stuck it under the bridge. Nooo problem! Nobody even paid any attention to us. After I got back up to the truck, Jeannie and I just did a little neck-ing. Kind of a cover-up job." He smiled over at me slyly.

"Come on, Bill. Now stop that—it's none of their business!" Jeannie shot him a dirty look, and both of us guys laughed.

Bill took his foot down from the bumper and sat down on the tail-gate next to Jeannie. She tried to scoot away from him, but Jen was in the way. He quickly put his arm around her and snuggled her into his side. He was wearing his cowboy hat, and he snapped it back on his head with a flick of his right index finger. He bent down, turning his head into the front of Jeannie's face giving her a quick peck on the cheek. Jeannie blushed a little and all was forgiven.

"Have you seen any sign of Slick, Howie, or any of the rest of the gang?" I asked.

"Nope," Bill replied. "Not a hide nor hair of anybody."

"You guys want to walk around with us while we go get our tickets for tonight's show? Maybe if we stick around a while, they'll show up."

"Ya want to go with 'em, hon?" Bill asked Jeannie.

"Sure," she answered, "but you'd better get me back pretty soon. I don't want my daddy to get suspicious."

"Shall do."

The four of us walked around to the front of the movie house where I bought two tickets for the eight o'clock show and headed back to the parking lot. Still nobody else had showed up.

"Hey, Rock," Bill said, "you two don't forget to keep it mum to Jen's folks about me and Jeannie or I'll tan both of your hides to the shed." He wagged his right index finger at me as he ushered Jeannie into the driver's side of his pickup. Just before he climbed in beside her, he said they'd see us later at the Pard.

Bill and his girl backed the truck out and turned to leave the parking lot. Both of them waved good-bye over their shoulders through the back window. A Waylon Jennings tune could be heard as they drove away. Jennifer and I jumped in Ironsides and left.

"I sure hope the other guys made it all right," I said.

"We'll find out at the Pard tonight. You'd better get me home, too, Rock. You know, I've still got to see if Mom and Dad will let me stay out 'til one o'clock."

"They've got to let you go, Jen! They've got to! You've *got* to be there tonight. It'll be a real night to remember."

Jen reached over and turned on the radio. The Surfaris were playing "Wipe Out."

Chapter Twenty-Two

"Good evening, Rock," Mr. Lucas said warmly as he answered the door. "Come on in. Jennifer will be right down." He pushed open the storm door as I backed up a bit to make room on the narrow front porch step for the door to swing past me. I moved around and stepped up into house past Mr. Lucas, whose back was pressed against the hinges of both doors, his arms extended out holding both doors open.

I walked through the front hall's archway into the dinning room. Sticking her head around the corner of the doorway, on the opposite side of the room, Mrs. Lucas waved me over to join her in the kitchen. "Got plenty of extra chicken and potatoes if you'd like some, Rock," she said. "Jennifer will be down in a minute or so."

"No thanks, Mrs. Lucas. I just finished eating a big dinner at home and I'm stuffed." I smiled at her and patted my stomach.

I heard the front door shut behind him. Jennifer's father came up behind me and put a big hand on my left shoulder. "Come on into the living room, son, and have a seat while you wait."

I threw another "thank you" in Mrs. Lucas's direction and turned to follow Jen's dad into the adjacent room. Her father motioned me over to an overstuffed brown couch along the wall as he settled into his well-worn brown leather recliner. I sat on the edge of one of the corner cushions on the couch. It was so soft that I sat down so low that my knees ended up almost touching my chin. I immediately scooted back into the center of the cushion and leaned back into the couch. My knees were still elevated nearly up to my chest. I tried to relax, which was almost impossible. Mr. Lucas looked straight ahead at the General Electric color television set, which was at the far end of the room against the wall. The introductory music to *Bonanza* was playing as the four stars of the popular western program were riding their horses into the Lucas's living room. Ben Cartright, and his three sons, Hoss, Little Joe, and Adam, were introduced to us as their real names flashed in bold letters across the screen. Mr. Lucas turned to look at me.

"Jennifer asked us at dinner if she could stay out 'til one so you two could go out with Bill and his date to a double feature at the Chief."

"Yes, sir."

"We told her it would be OK this time, but we'd like to know your plans a little sooner if you want to stay out past midnight again."

"Yes, sir, we sure will. I didn't—"

Jen's father held up his hand interrupting me.

"Jennifer's mother and I just want you to know that we like you very much, Rock. We just want to make sure that you know we respect you and that we insist that you treat our daughter with the respect she deserves."

I was looking down at the floor in front of me, then turned my head up and looked Mr. Lucas right in the eyes. "Yes, sir," I said. "I know that. And I sure will. And I want to thank you for letting Jen—I mean Jennifer—stay out a little later tonight. I promise I will have her home no later than one o'clock."

Jen's father nodded his head in approval and looked back toward the TV. Jennifer could be heard coming down the stairs.

"Hi, Rock. Did Daddy tell you it was all right for me to stay out until one?"

"Yup. Sure did."

Jennifer bounced around the corner of the living room entrance at the bottom of the stairs and came up behind her father's chair. She wrapped her arms around him from the back and kissed him gently on top of his head. Her dad reached up with his right hand and patted her arm in appreciation. "You kids be careful and have fun."

"We will, Daddy, and thanks a lot." She kissed the top of his head again and gestured for me to get up. I grasped her hand and got up, thanking Mr. Lucas once again. Her father glanced over and smiled up at me, then turned back to watch *Bonanza*.

I let Jen move ahead of me out the room. Just before we opened the front door to leave, we peeked around the archway of the dining room to say good-bye to her mother.

"You kids be careful and have a good time at the movies"

"OK, Mom. We will. Love you!"

As Old Ironsides pulled away from the curb, I said to Jen, "Man, your folks are super. I was so worried that you wouldn't be able to go out tonight for some reason or other, but you're here and the night of our lives is about to begin!" I reached around Jen's shoulders and pulled her in close.

The rest of the gang was already at the Pard when we arrived, and they were huddled around the back of Bill's pickup. They all turned and watched as I pulled up and parked next to Slick's Chevy. I held the door open as Jennifer scooted over across the seat and got out. She went over to join Jeannie and I moved to the outside center of the gang.

"Well, did you guys get your cans placed under your bridges?" I asked the guys. "Anybody have any problems?"

"Nope, everything is cool," Slick said. "We're ready to go. Let's do it!"

"Yeah, let's torch those bastards!" Zero shouted.

"Goddamnit, Zero! Shut the fuck up! The whole parking lot could've heard you!" Slick said shoving a stiff finger into Zero's chest. The rest of the gang stared at Zero, then leaned in toward him to emphasize their point.

There was a short moment of silence as everybody slowly looked around at each other. Jen's and Jeannie's eyes were focused on the entire group. I glanced over and made direct eye contact with Jen. Without taking my eyes off of hers, I quietly said, "Well, boys, we all know the jobs we have to do." A slight smile was on my face and I turned back, looking each gang member in the eye. "As soon as your mission is accomplished, take off and head up to the cave. Good luck and see you in a few hours."

I stuck out my right hand and shook Bill's first. Following suit, all the other members started shaking hands with each other, then split up into their respective groups and headed for their cars. I waved for Jen to join me, and Jeannie moved around to the passenger side of Bill's truck, opened the door, and hopped in next to her boyfriend. Just as I was about to get into Ironsides I looked over the car's roof at Bill as Bill gave the thumbs-up sign and smiled back at me through the truck window.

I put Ironsides in reverse and just before I started to back up, I leaned down and gave Jennifer a kiss. "Here we go. Are you ready?"

Jen didn't reply, she only looked straight ahead. I backed up, then shifted into drive and pulled out onto Eighth Street and headed south toward Brookshire.

Chapter *Twenty-Three*

Just as I was coming up to the stoplight at Eighth Street and Cheyenne Road, I saw Bill turn his truck left toward Alsace Way. I turned and pulled up behind him.

"Are you and Bill gonna take both vehicles?" Jen asked.

"Damn, never even thought about that," I said. "We'll figure out something when we get to the bridge. We won't be able to park close to the bridge or somebody will stop to check it out to see if anything's wrong. I think we can park along one of the streets close to the bridge, and it'll be all right. I'll check with Blackburn when we get there and decide then."

A few minutes later I saw Bill's right taillight blinking, indicating that the Alsace Way turn was coming up. I popped my turn signal up for a right hand turn and followed right behind Bill. It was only a couple of blocks to the bridge, and Bill turned his truck over to the edge of the curb and waited for us to pull up right behind him. As soon as Ironsides pulled up behind him, Bill got out and walked back to my window. I rolled my window down and Bill leaned into the window, putting both of his elbows on the window ledge.

"Jeannie and I were talking about what we were gonna do with your car. I know we planned on using my truck."

"Yeah, Jen brought up the same thing. What I suggest is we just take my car and park it over there around the corner of Cottonwood Lane. I don't think anybody will even notice it there. What do you think?" I looked at Bill, then back at Jen to see what she thought of the idea.

Jen nodded her head in approval and Bill agreed.

"Why don't we just use it ourselves? Jeannie and I could just hop in it right after we torch the bridge and then meet you guys over at the Pard," Jen said, waving toward Jeannie to come join us. Jeannie saw her wave and got out of the truck and came around the passenger side of the Ironsides and slid in next to Jen. "What's up?" she asked.

Bending down so he could see Jeannie better, Bill said, "We're discussing what to do with Rock's car. What Jen thought is that you two gals could use it to get away right after you burn the bridge and that way the other fellas wouldn't have to come all the way down here to pick you up. We'll just pick a time for you to torch the bridge that will come pretty close to the same time the other bridges are torched. What do you think?"

"Gill and Rick are supposed to pick us up. How are they gonna know that they shouldn't come and get us?" Jeannie asked.

"Yeah, how are they gonna know what to do?" Jen said, looking at Jeannie, then turning to Bill and me.

"Hmmm, good question. Guess that won't work," I said, leaning forward and wrapping both my arms over the top of steering wheel with my hands clasped together.

"Wait a minute," Bill said. "Rick and Gill are going to be at Sully's gas station when we meet the other guys, waiting for Howie or Jim to call us after they shoot the first light out. We can tell them then. Everything will be cool, no sweat. That will work, and you gals can sky out as soon as you take care of the bridge."

Both Jeannie and Jen looked at the two boys with puzzled looks on their faces. Jen spoke up first. "OK, so we'll get of out here right after we burn the bridge and meet you guys at the Pard. But how are we gonna know when to do it?"

I leaned back away from the steering wheel. Looking straight ahead and at no one in particular, I said, "All hell will start breaking loose in about half an hour, around ten or so. If we figured it will take the teams about an hour and a half to black out their quadrants, that'll take the clock down to about 11:30. If you two girls plan on torching this bridge between 11:30 and 11:45, you'll be right on time." I looked first over at Bill, then turned to the girls. "Yeah, that will work."

"Shit!" Jeannie said. "Bill, I don't know about Jennifer, but I'm scared to death. What happens if we screw up?"

Bill leaned back away from the car door and walked around to Jeannie's side of the car and opened the door. Jeannie got right out and Bill held her tight in her arms.

"Hey, you don't have to go through with this if you don't want to," Bill said. "Rock and I can take care of it if you want." He was holding his girl tight and lifted his eyes to look over her shoulder into the car toward Jennifer and me. By this time I moved closer to Jen and had my arm up over her shoulders and was holding her close. Both of us guys were looking past our girls into each other's eyes. Both of us knew, without saying, that we would honor whatever the girls decided to do.

"Bill and I will go along with whatever you and Jeannie want. If you don't want to go ahead with this we'll understand," I said.

Bill nodded in agreement with what I'd just said. Jen moved away from me, and I moved my arm from around her shoulders up to the back of the seat. She turned to look at her friend. Jeannie turned and scooted back into the front seat of the car next to Jen. The two girls sat there looking at each for a moment.

"What do you want to do, Jeannie? I'll go along with whatever you decide."

Jeannie held both of her hands in the middle of her lap. She looked down at them, then after a moment she looked back up and at Bill. "I'm just scared that something will go really wrong and we'll all get into big trouble. If we get caught, I don't know what will happen. I know that, besides all the trouble we'd get in, my daddy would never let me see you again. Ever!" She stopped for a moment, then continued, "I don't think I could ever live with myself if I knew I would never be able to see you again, Bill." Then she turned her head back down and looked in her lap and began crying. Bill was bending down to move in to give her a hug when Jen motioned for him to stay back. Jen put her arms around her friend and hugged her close.

"It's OK, Jeannie. We don't have to do this."

Jeannie started to sit up and was wiping the tears from her eyes with the back of both her hands. Sniffling up the last of her tears she pulled herself together and said with a thick voice, "No, I'll be all right. I'm just a little nervous, that's all. We need to get going or you guys will miss the meeting at Sully's. I'll do it if you're still willing to go through with it, Jen."

"OK, girl. Let's do it!" Jen said, shaking her friend lovingly with her arms around her. "You and I can do this and everything will be just fine. Let's do it"

Jeannie moved away from her friend and got out of the car to Bill. She moved into his waiting arms, and he hugged her tight, then tilted her head up to meet his lips.

I moved back over to Jen as she turned into my arms and both couples were holding each other in a warm, kissing embrace. A few moments passed before each couple separated.

"OK, ladies, let's get Operation Blackout Brookshire underway," I said. "Jen and I will park around the corner over there on Cottonwood and we'll be right back."

In a couple of minutes Jen and I were walking back to the bridge where our friends were waiting for us.

"Why don't you two go hop into Rock's pony and go over to the Pard for some fries and a Coke?" Bill said. "It'll be a good hour and a half before you'll need to get back here. Besides, it wouldn't look too good for you two girls to be parked over there for that length of time, and the time will go much faster if you go out and do something between now and then. How does that sound?"

"Sounds good to us," the girls said in unison.

"Now, Bill and I want you to be super careful when you get ready to light the match to this torch. Remember to soak those timbers under the bridge with the gas we have hidden right under there," I said, indicating where the can was and pointing toward the timbers.

"Yup," Bill agreed. "And when you decide to light the torch make sure you're way back from the bridge because the fumes from gas can ignite—make sure you're back right about where we're right now before you strike the match. Right after the torch catches, just throw it as hard and as far as you can right under the bridge and run like crazy to the car and get the heck out of here as fast as you can. Once you get on Cheyenne Road don't speed, just drive normally and take your time heading to the Pard. I know you're gonna be nervous and scared, but just hold yourselves together and everything will be just fine. If Rock and I aren't there yet, don't worry—we'll be along in short order. Nothing is going to go wrong and we'll see you in a little over two hours. Everything OK?"

The two girls looked at each other and each took a deep breath. Jeannie nodded her head in approval to Jen and shrugged her shoulders. Jen looked at both of the boys and said, "OK, guys. We're ready. Now you fellas better get going or you'll miss the show."

Chapter *Twenty-Four*

I sat with Bill in his pickup as the girls turned out of Cottonwood Lane and headed back to Cheyenne Road. When Ironsides turned left and moved out of sight we pulled away from the curb and headed across the Alsace bridge up the hill toward Sully's gas station.

When we rounded the corner of Blake and Pine, the other two cars were already parked next to the public phone booth just to the right of the main station building. Bill pulled his truck up alongside Gill's car and turned the motor off. The four other boys were milling around in front of Slick's Chevy, which was parked right in front of the phone booth.

Slick looked over at me as we walked over to join our buddies. "Man," he said nervously, "we thought you guys might've chickened out. What happened? You have some trouble with the girls? And before you ask, nope, we haven't heard a word from Howie or Jim. We figure they should be shooting the light out just about now and the phone will ring in just a few minutes."

While Slick, Rick, Jerry, Gill, Bill, and I were waiting around the phone booth at Sully's, Howie and Jim were just pulling up and under the streetlight at the corner of Swan and Long's Peak Road. As he told us later, another car was just turning onto Swan, and Howie stepped on the accelerator and moved down the block, looking in his rearview mirror, watching the other car as it disappeared around the next corner down the street.

"Damn!" Howie had said to Jim. "That was too damn close for comfort. I'll turn around at the next corner, and when we get back under the light you lean out the window and shoot that damn light out as quick as you can. If you miss I ain't gonna turn around so you can have another chance, so make it good."

Jim had his window already rolled down and the barrel of his .22 Remington pump rifle was just barely out the window. Howie said Jim didn't say a word as Howie wheeled the car around and headed back to the bright shining streetlight on the corner.

When the car was about fifty yards from the light, Howie swerved over to the left lane so Jim could lean out the window and shoulder the tiny rifle for a good shot. When the car was about thirty feet away and at a slight angle from the base of the light, Jim told him to slow down and stop. Howie eased the car up and brought it to a jerky stop.

"Jesus, slam on the brakes why don't you?" Jim's rifle bumped against the window vent with a clicking sound that metal against metal makes.

"SHOOT! SHOOT!" Howie screamed.

Jim was leaning halfway out the window. His cheek was resting tight on the rifle's stock with the barrel pointed up at the bulb under the silver steel hood of the overhanging streetlight. Lining up the front and rear sights along the top of the barrel, Jim slowly squeezed the trigger and the tiny rifle jumped just a bit against his shoulder as the loud crack of the shot rang out. An instant later the big bulb made a loud popping noise, flickered just a bit and went dark. Almost simultaneously with the sound of the rifle shot and the pop of the bulb, tiny pieces of broken glass rained down on the top and hood of the car, and Howie slammed the accelerator pedal hard to the floor. The rear tires of the Chevy squealed, laying a thirty-foot strip of rubber as the car jumped forward down Long's Peak Road. The jolt of the car moving forward slammed Jim back against the back frame of the car's door. Within seconds he was back inside, rolling his window up and putting the rifle down, lengthwise under the front seat of the car.

"HOLY SHIT! Did you see that son of a bitch explode? That was the coolest sound in the world! We're really doin' it! Operation Blackout Brookshire is officially on its goddamned way!"

Howie told us that he felt like he was driving the Chevy as though he were in the race of his life. His knuckles were marble white as he gripped the steering wheel. And while Jim was jumping around next to him shouting at the top of his lungs, Howie was leaning into the steering wheel and almost whispering to himself, "Oh shit, oh shit, oh shit…"

Jim started to quiet down when he noticed how far they'd driven since the shot.

"Howie! Howie! Slow down before we get caught for speeding. Did you forget? We've got to turn around and park somewhere close to that light and wait for the repair guys to show up, so slow down and turn this hunk of shit around." He looked over at Howie. "Hey, man, you all right?"

"Yeah, I'm fine. When you squeezed off that shot, it just scared the piss out of me. I never thought it was gonna be so loud. And that light— Jesus it sounded like an M-80 when it blew up! I'm doing better now, though. You're right, we have to go back and park where the power people can't see us and call the other guys to let them know everything went right on the money. I'll bet they're shittin' shingles just waiting to see if we chickened out or not. Man, wait until they find out the big operation is on its way. Fuckin' A, this is really a pump."

Howie's Chevy eased up under the overhanging branches of a huge cottonwood just around the corner and about halfway down the block from the dark street corner where the arching tall steel streetlight hung, looking like a huge branchless hangman's tree. Just seconds after Howie cut the lights on his car, he saw two bright headlights appear from the darkness about two blocks away. Both boys were completely silent as the lights grew bigger and closer. When the vehicle lights slowed as they approached the darkened streetlight, the boys knew it was the repair crew. Sure enough, the crew truck stopped right under the darkened streetlight, and two men got out on either side of the power company truck. One of the men moved to the back of the truck and started to unload the huge ladder that was strapped to the top of the truck.

"That's them," Jim whispered.

"Yeah," Howie replied, "let's make like horse shit and hit the road. I'm gonna turn down this street so they don't see who we are and head over to the phone booth and call the guys."

When the phone rang in the booth next to Sully's garage all six of us jumped at the same time.

"Slick, get the damn phone!"

"No, you get it, Gill!"

"Well, for Christ's sake. Somebody get that damn thing!" Jerry said.

While the rest of us were standing around looking at the phone booth, Bill opened the accordion doors and picked up the phone on its fourth ring. Before he could get a single word out, the shouts from Jim came from the other end.

"We did it! We shot the fuckin' light out and it blew up like a bomb!"

Bill motioned to the other guys standing around the front of the booth that it was a thumbs-up, and he said that Howie and Jim blew the fucker from here to kingdom come.

"Did the repair crew show up or not? Yeah. Super. We're gonna head out right away, and you guys are gonna go back and blast that son of a bitch again, aren't you? OK. Let's get this fucker rollin'. Good luck and see you two in a couple of hours at the Pard. Remember to take it easy, but do your best to shoot out every goddamned light that you can. Bye."

Bill hung up the phone and pushed his way past the other boys, who were crowded around the front of the phone booth.

"The little sonsabitches did it!" Bill reported to us. "Jim said the bulb goes off like a bomb when you hit it, then it flickers a little bit just before it goes out completely. He also said the repair guys were there just a couple of minutes ago and were getting ready to fix the light. They're gonna head back there and if the coast is clear they're gonna shoot it out again and start working their way over to the bridge. Let's go, men. We've got a job to do."

"Damn, we almost forgot to tell you," I said, grabbing hold of Gill's shoulder holding him back. "You and Rick don't have to worry about picking the girls up. We left my car with them, and they'll torch the bridge as soon as you guys cross it, then they're gonna meet us back at the Pard."

"No sweat, Rock," Gill said. "That's fine with us, and we'll stop to help your ladies out right after we cross the bridge." Gill looked at both of his buddies and gave them a wink. "Don't worry, studs, we'll take care of your women for you." With that said he jumped into his car as Bill and I flipped Gill and Rick the bird.

As the other two cars backed up and headed to their respective quadrants, Bill leaned over the top of his truck just as I was about to get in. "Here we go, mother-fucker!" he sang. Then we both climbed into the cab of the truck, backed it out of Sully's lot, and headed out.

Chapter *Twenty-Five*

When Howie turned his Chevy onto Swan the power company repair crew was just putting the ladder back on top of the truck. By the time they spotted the repair truck it was too late to turn around so they just kept going. As they were approaching the truck the fellow on the driver's side was waving his arm up and down indicating that he wanted the boys to slow down and stop.

"What the fuck do you think they want, Howie? You s'pose they saw us when we drove away? Shit, we're screwed!"

"Just cool it, Jim. Roll down your window and just act like nothing happened and ask them if they need any help. Relax and hold your cool, they don't suspect a thing. Probably just want to tell us what happened."

Howie pulled his car over next to the repair truck as Jim rolled down the window. The repairman was a big fella and looked like he was in his mid-forties, dressed in blue jeans and a Western shirt with the company logo printed just above the left shirt pocket and "Bob" embroidered just above the logo. When Howie stopped the car Bob came over and put his hand on the window sill and bent over to look inside the car.

"You guys need some help or something?" Jim said, looking Bob right in the eyes.

"Naw, not really. Guess some kids got a wild hair up their ass and decided it would be cool to shoot out the streetlight. You fellas haven't seen any kids running around here this evening, have you?"

Jim turned and looked over at Howie, then turned back to Bob. "Nope, haven't seen a thing. We were driving around here just a while ago and the light was working fine. Howie and I were just up visiting our girls."

The repairman put a smile on his face, reached in the car and grabbed Jim by the shoulder with a firm grip that made Jim squirm a bit. "Now, you boys keep a sharp eye on those ladies—they can be a bunch of trouble," he said, giving Jim a wink, then pulling his hand back. "I'd appreciate it if you'd keep a sharp eye out for some foolhardy kids, and if you see some give us a call and let us know. Or let the sheriff know. Thanks now, and you fellas have a good evening."

Jim was nodding his head in agreement, and Howie leaned over to look at Bob. "We sure will." The boys said in unison. "See ya later."

Howie eased the car away from the repair truck and headed straight down Swan.

"Now what the fuck do we do?" Jim said, looking straight ahead. "We can go right back there and blast that light out now. But those guys will know for sure we did it."

"No, they won't. Jesus, what a shit head. We'll just go over a few blocks and give those guys some time to head back to their office. It only took them about five minutes to get here after we shot out the light, so it'll only take them about the same time to get back to their office. Let's head over and take out the light on Acorn Street and then come back and take out this light again. Besides, the other guys will have a few lights out by the time they get to their office and they'll probably head out in a completely different direction."

"OK, let's get going and get the hell out of here," Jim said, then he slugged Howie in the shoulder and smiled. "Shit head."

Gill pulled his car up and under their third streetlight. Rick leaned out of his window, took careful aim, and let fire. The rifle cracked and the bright bulb popped loudly and slowly fizzled to darkness. Moving around the corner, they moved on to their fourth light and repeated the process. Both boys were laughing out loud with each light they blasted.

"God, this is a gas!" Rick said as he reloaded more .22 shells in the clip of his Savage rifle. "At this rate we'll be done in no time. And have you noticed how dark it is behind us? Damn, this place is going to look like midnight when we get done!"

"Yeah, if we don't get caught. You just keep blasting those lights and let's get out of here before somebody spots us!"

Slick and Jerry were moving right along shooting out every light along their quadrant's stretch of Penrose Boulevard. Jerry was shooting a single-shot Crosman .22 caliber pellet gun. He had just pulled the bolt back and was slipping in another pellet when they came up to the corner of Penrose and Will Rogers Road. This was the last light on the far end of their quadrant before they turned and moved down a block to work their way back. Slick eased the car up under the light, and Jerry took careful aim and the light shattered then went dark.

Bill and I were doing the same thing in our quadrant. We had already shot out eleven lights, and slowly but surely the hilltop community of Brookshire was going black.

Chapter *Twenty-Six*

Bob and Chuck, the two repairmen, just walked into the office of the Brookshire Power Company Headquarters.

Bob was pouring himself a cup of coffee from the silver-plated Westinghouse percolator. His partner was settling into his oak swivel chair behind his desk. He turned his chair around to check the board.

"What the hell? Hey, Bob, come look at this. Something must be screwed up with this thing. It's showing nearly thirty lights out. And, hey, there go two more and another over on Pecos, Pine Cone, and Marble and—Bob, what the fuck's going on?"

"Son of a bitch!" Bob yelped. "I can see from here. Hey, there go two, no, three and two more over there! Hell, Chuck, this can't be right. There has to be something wrong with this thing. Let's just cool it a bit—there can't be that many lights out. Something must have shorted out with the board. Why don't you just come over here and get yourself a hot cup of Joe. We'll see if we can check out the board as soon as we sit back and enjoy the coffee for a minute or two."

As the two men sat back in their chairs they just stared up at the big troubleshooting board on the wall behind Chuck's desk, watching the indicator lights going out one after the other all across the board. As they watched the board slowly go black, Bob said, "Lookit that, would ya? They seem to be going out one at a time in all four sections of the hill! Looks like they're going dark in perfect sequence down four separate streets at a time. There, look at that, see? There goes one on Pine Cone and one on Walnut—and looky over here. Look at that, would ya? Lights are out all along Penrose, Pine Cone, Will Rogers, and, hey, there goes two more. One way over here and one down here on Alsace Way." He looked over at Chuck, who was getting back up out of his chair. Looking at his partner and pointing up at the light board following the little bulbs going out from one side of the board to the other, he turned and looked at Bob. Both men had scrunched-up faces and questioning looks in their eyes. In a soft voice Chuck said, "What in God's name is going on here?"

Bob turned and looked back at the ever-darkening board. "I sure as hell don't have a clue, but we'd better head out to see what's going on. I can't help but think that something is wrong with this damn thing. There's no shittin' way that many lights could be out. Would you look at that? According to this damn thing the light over at Swan and Long's Peak is out again. It just can't be, but we'd better check it out."

The two men put their coffee cups over next to the silver coffeepot, grabbed their jackets, and headed out to their truck.

As they turned out of the power company's service yard, they headed north. They circled around in front of the Brookshire Hotel, where the road encompassed the entire resort. When they turned off the street that circled the resort and headed down Stover Road, Bob pulled the truck over to the curb and stopped. Both men just looked straight ahead in complete disbelief. For as far as they could see, the entire street in front of them was completely dark except for an occasional front porch light on a house.

"Would you look at that! Not one fuckin' light! Hell, the only thing that looks lit are the stars," Chuck whispered more to himself than to his partner.

The truck pulled away from the curb and slowly moved down Stover Road. As they came to each intersection, they looked right and left only to see complete darkness and not a single street lamp shining.

"Slow down next to this next light so I can look around. There has to be an answer for all of this."

When Bob pulled over, Chuck got out and walked around with his flashlight, first shining the beam up toward the street lamp. After studying the empty housing for a moment he heard the crunch of glass under his feet. He moved the flashlight's beam down toward his feet. Tiny sparkles of glass flashed back into his eyes, reflecting back from the bright beam of light. He kicked some of the pieces with the sole of his boot, then turned back to face Bob in the truck. Still walking slowly, he returned to the truck and opened the door and got in, his flashlight still on.

"Looks like the same thing happened to this light as what happened to the one we repaired on the corner of Swan. Someone shot the damn thing."

"What in the hell do you think is going on here, Chuck? There ain't no damn way this could've been done by some kids. If the light board's right back at the office, this is happening all over the damn place. Just can't be kids!"

Both men just sat in the cab of their truck and looked expressionlessly at each other. With the light of the flashlight casting a yellow glow throughout the cab, their faces took on an eerie glow.

"We'd better get back to the office and see if we can figure this sucker out. There has to be a simple answer to what's going on. There's no way someone is running around shooting out every one of these lights just for kicks," Bob said, looking at Chuck's glowing face. "Is there?"

"Let's get 'er back to the office right now!"

When the two men pulled into the yard of the power company office, the sheriff's car was already parked in the lot. The two men got out of their truck and walked into the office. Daddy Bruce was sitting in Bob's chair, leaning back against a filing cabinet with one foot up on the edge of his desk. He was looking at the darkening light board, never even looking over toward the two men when they walked in.

"Well, boys, what the hell is happening here? When I got the first couple of calls at the department, I tried to give you fellas a jingle but couldn't get you, so I decided to drive over here to see if you were outside. On my way over I decided to go around a few blocks out of the way and every goddamned light I saw was blown to smithereens." He took his foot off the desk and put it back on the floor and tilted the chair back and leaned on the desk folding his chubby hands together in front of himself. He looked away from the board over to the two men standing to his left. Slowly spacing his words so they wouldn't be misunderstood, he looked both men in the eyes. "What in the devil's name is going on here? Now it looked like to me that those lights I saw were shot out, but I just want to know if you boys have another solution as to what is happening here."

The men looked at each other, then turned to look down at the sheriff. Bob finally said, "Damn it, Sheriff, I know it doesn't sound feasible, but it sure as hell looks like somebody is out there shooting every light out from one end of Brookshire to the other. We just got back from checking out Stover and a couple of the blocks parallel to it, and every damn light that we could see was out and each one looked like it was shot all to hell. Earlier this evening we had a light go out over on Swan and Long's Peak, and when we got back to the office after repairing it, we saw the bulbs on the board going out all over the place. We didn't think that could actually happen so we took off to check it out, and sure as hell, the lights were out, as you say, shot all to hell."

"Well, boys, you're the experts here, so what do you think is happening? Think we got a loony out there or is it something else? There's got to be an answer somewhere. If we don't figure it out pretty damn soon, the whole goddamn hill will be black as midnight." Turning his head back to the board on the wall, he said,

"Lookit that! There goes a half-dozen more! And over there. Whoever it is, they're blowing the holy shit out of every streetlight on the hill."

The sheriff was still leaning forward with his hands folded together on the desk, and the two men standing next to him were watching the tiny bulbs on the board slowly but methodically going out one at a time. All three men were slowly shaking their heads back and forth in complete disbelief at what they were watching on the board.

"If you really watch how those lights are going out, they're all following a specific pattern," Chuck said, moving over toward the board on the wall. He lifted his right hand, and with his finger he started tracing the path of each bulb as it went out, "Watch this now. See, whoever it is, they're moving right along Blue Jay, and over here they're working along Willow. And look, these guys are moving straight right down Flicker, and over here the lights are going out all along Starlight Drive."

"Son of a bitch if you don't have something there, Chuck." Bob moved over to the other side of the board and was pointing and tracing the paths of lights going out where Chuck followed them. "Yup. Looks like to me they're moving in a pattern that'll take them to the north and down the face of the hill toward town. At least these three areas are moving that way." Bob shifted over toward the area that was covered by Bill and Rock. "See here? These guys look like they're moving east. I think they're going to finish up somewhere over here by the Penrose bridge and will probably cut out of here on the highway and head into town from there.

"If you check this out, whoever these guys are, they're the closest to us right now and are going to end up right at the Seven Falls Road bridge." He turned back to the sheriff, paused, and said, "Right now it looks like they're going to have every streetlight shot out across the entire hill in less than half an hour. If we're going to have a chance to catch these sonsabitches at all, we're gonna have to move fast and I mean right now. There are less than twenty lights left burning in each sector."

Bruce backed away a couple of steps from the other two men. He pointed first at Bob, then waved his hand over at Chuck. "OK, you two guys get in your truck right now and head over to where these guys are heading to Seven Falls Road. Shit, I'm short-handed." He kind of rolled his eyes and said, "Delbert. Deputy Delbert? Oh, well. I'll get him on the radio and send him up here to see if he can find these guys. I'll head east toward the Penrose bridge to see if I can corner those bastards." He paused. "These crazy fools are armed, so you guys be damned careful. Does your radio work in your truck?"

Both men nodded yes.

"If you suspect any trouble at all, you call me at this frequency *immediately* and get the hell out of there. If you can, find out the make of the car and get the license plate number and don't try anything heroic. Just get that information if you can and get the hell out of there." The sheriff shook both men's hands and turned quickly toward the door.

"Let's move!"

Chapter *Twenty-Seven*

"Hit it, Jim! Come on, shoot the damn thing!" Howie shouted as he pulled up to and under the bright streetlight, "This is the last one on this street and we're heading to the last block."

Right after Jim's gun cracked from the shot, the light shattered. Before it was completely out, Howie slammed the accelerator of the Chevy to the floor, shifted quickly into second gear, and peeled around the corner. Jim brought the gun back inside and was reloading .22 shells into the tube magazine on the bottom of the barrel. Howie had the Chevy in third gear and had to downshift when the car approached the next corner. When the downshift caught, the tires screeched, bringing the car's speed from forty-five miles an hour down to thirty almost immediately.

"Damn it, Howie, cool it! You almost made me shove the barrel of the gun through the windshield. Jesus!"

"Fuck you! We have to get moving, so just do your job and shoot that damn light out. If we don't get moving, we're gonna get our asses caught!"

The Chevy moved up under the corner light and, without coming to a complete stop, Jim leaned out the window, aimed, and squeezed the trigger. Almost simultaneously with the report of the gun the light blew up and went dark. Before all the shattered glass dropped to the pavement, Howie's car was moving down the block to the next light.

"Move it, Howie! We've only got two more lights to go. Let's get 'em and get across that bridge NOW!"

With two more lights to go, Howie slammed on the brakes twenty feet from the next light, leaving a ten-foot strip of rubber on the asphalt. Jim pointed the rifle upward and the light above him disappeared.

"Look! There's those bastards right up there! Did you just see that light go out right after they pulled away?" Chuck said, pointing straight ahead of the two men in the truck. "Come on, Bob. Let's get 'em!"

Bob put his foot to the floor and the truck lurched forward, picking up speed fast as they headed straight toward the Chevy, five blocks in front of them.

"Oh, shit!" Howie shouted. "There's a car coming up behind us about four or five blocks back and, man, they're movin'!"

Jim turned around and looked over the back of the front seat. "Fuckin' A, you're right! And they're gaining on us fast, Howie. We better screw the last light and get out of here."

"Fuck 'em. I'm gonna pull up to that last light. The turn to go across the bridge is right there."

"Hey, man, we can't do that! Those sonsabitches are coming on strong and they'll see us! Goose it, goddamnit! Let's get the fuck out of here! Forget the damn—Howie, it's the repair truck!"

The truck was less than two blocks back when the Chevy came to a screeching halt directly under the light on the corner. A big cloud of dust came up behind it from the car sliding on the loose gravel on the pavement.

"Get this hunk of—"

"SHUT UP AND JUST SHOOT THE FUCKIN' LIGHT—NOW!"

A split second after Jim's gun went off, Howie slammed his right foot to the floor. The tires of the Chevy spun and squealed, spitting gravel and a huge cloud of dust into the air behind it. When the tires finally caught on the asphalt, the car shot forward and fishtailed around the corner. Within seconds they shot across the Seven Falls Road Bridge.

As soon as they crossed the bridge, Howie stomped on the brakes and turned the steering wheel as hard as he could to the right. The car swerved and went into a broadside slide as it rounded the corner onto Cheyenne Road. Zero was running out from under the bridge just as the car straightened out and slid to a stop five feet away from the curb.

"TORCH IT! TORCH IT NOW!" Both Howie and Jim were out of the car and running directly toward Zero, who came to a halt and started to run back to the bridge, then back toward the other two boys, his arms flapping up and down. He looked at both of the boys running at him. "Now? You want me to torch it now?" The boy started to spin in circles like one of his feet was nailed to the ground. He couldn't figure out which way to go.

Howie and Jim ran right past him, down the slope heading under the bridge.

"Fuck, Zero, can't you do anything right? There's a couple of guys from the power company chasing us, and they'll be here any minute!" Howie shouted just as he disappeared under the bridge. "Where in the hell's the torch! ZERO, WHERE'S THE DAMNED TORCH?"

Jim was halfway down the slope to the underside of the bridge when he turned back to get Zero's help. All he could see was space between him and the car. "HE'S GONE! ZERO CHICKENED OUT AND SPLIT!"

Looking back once more to see if he could find Zero, Jim ran down the slope and almost stumbled when Howie grabbed him by his arm and turned him around.

"I found the torch, and at least that lousy son of a bitch dumped the gas on the bridge and there's some on the torch! Get back up to the road. Let's torch this bridge and get our butts out of here!"

Just as the boys turned to look back at the bridge, there were two headlights coming straight at them from the other side, about half a block away.

Jim was fumbling in his left shirt pocket and found a book of matches. He pulled them out, folded back the top flap, ripped a single match out, and struck it on the graphite strip. The match lit, but he dropped it at his feet. In a panic he ripped a half-dozen matches from the book, struck them all along the graphite strip. They burst into flame and Howie swung the rag-wrapped end of the stick into the flame that Jim held out to him. The torch burst into flame. Howie held it for a minute, mesmerized by the flame.

"Throw the damn thing, Howie! THROW IT!"

Howie swung the torch down and over the back of his shoulder. His arm came back quickly over the top and the torch went sailing, end over end, right into the dark cavern under the bridge. Even before the torch hit the ground, the hot flame ignited the gas fumes that hung heavy in the air and the bridge exploded into a burning inferno, shooting out from under both sides of the bridge and over a hundred feet into the air. Even though both of the boys had turned and started running back to their car, the blast from the gasoline igniting threw them flat on their faces into the grass and gravel berm fifty feet from their car.

When the bridge exploded a hundred yards in front of them, Bob's eyes widened in disbelief, and he slammed on the brakes of the truck. Both of the men's faces glowed orange from the bright, hot flame shooting up from all sides of the bridge.

"HOLY SHIT! HOLY SHIT! STOP THE TRUCK! STOP THE TRUCK!"

Chuck had both hands on the dashboard, bracing himself as all four wheels of the speeding truck locked up, sending it into a lurching slide, slowly swinging the truck into a broadside slide before sending them into the barrow ditch next to the road with a terrific impact. The truck's inertia sent it bouncing up and airborne until it came to rest fifty feet off the road. When the truck came to a standstill, both men leaned back and stared at each other. Chuck still had both hands on the dashboard, and Bob's hands were gripping the steering wheel as firmly as he could.

"Did you see that!?" Chuck said, slowly looking back toward the flaming bridge.

"Would you look at that! Those flames must be shooting up there over a hundred feet."

"What in hell are we supposed to do now? These boys are serious. Hey, did you get the make of their car before they turned down to the bridge?"

"Shit, Bob, we never did get close enough to see a thing. Besides, that cloud of dust they left when they cut out from under the last light made it impossible to see anything."

"There's nothing we can do here," Bob said, still looking at the flames reaching high into the night sky. "Get on the phone to the fire department and tell them to get over here as fast as they can. And we'd better get on the radio and tell Bruce what the hell happened here."

On the other side of the road, Howie and Jim scurried back to their feet and, running half bent over, got to the car and jumped in. Before Jim had his door closed Howie had the car turned on and in gear, leaving a tire-squealing spray of gravel and dirt behind them. Both boys rolled down their windows and while hollering at the top of their lungs extended their arms out the windows, flipping the bird back toward the burning bridge behind them. Howie could still see the flames shooting into the sky when he turned the car around a turn in the road. Slowing down to the speed limit, the Chevy headed east on Cheyenne

Boulevard. Both boys were singing as loud as they could along with "Hit the Road, Jack," which was blaring on the radio.

Glancing from the road in front of him and over to Jim, Howie looked at his buddy with a big smile on his face and said, "Let's haul ass over to the Will Rogers bridge and help Bobby torch that sucker."

With his fist closed tight, Jim thrust it hard in front of him toward the windshield while looking Howie in the eye. "Hit it! We've got another bridge to burn!"

The light just popped, sizzled, and went out, and Slick eased his car out from under the light and turned onto Stover Road just four blocks from the Stover Road bridge directly in front of them down the hill.

"Shoot, Slick, this has been a cinch! We've blasted at least forty lights to smithereens and haven't seen a soul."

"Yup, but we still have four to go, then we gotta get the hell out of here."

They were just getting ready to ease up under the light at the corner of Stover and Aspen when a police car pulled up to the intersection on their right.

"SHIT! There's Deputy Delbert! Turn right and go past him, then step on it and head up Aspen as fast as you can. That stupid sucker won't even know we went past him until we're halfway down the street. Hit the next left and goose it—we'll lose him before he realizes what happened and turns around."

Deputy Delbert pulled up the stop sign as the boys turned slowly and drove right past him. Both of them looked away so he wouldn't recognize them. He was talking on his radio, saying, "Yes, sir, I think I found where they left off. All the lights in this section are out except for about four more that I can see heading down to the Stover bridge." He paused as Slick turned and drove past him heading down Aspen. "A couple of kids just turned past me—and they just stepped on it and hit the next corner in a skid. That must be them, boss!"

Delbert sat there a few minutes just nodding in agreement to whatever was being said to him from the other end of the radio. Seconds later he threw the speaker down on the seat beside him, turned on the single multicolored light on the roof of his car, and switched on his siren. He pulled the car out into the intersection and squealed the tires as he spun around to head out in pursuit of the car that had disappeared around the corner behind him.

When Delbert hit the next corner he caught just a glimpse of the taillights as they turned left on the next corner. With siren blaring and the bubble light flashing on top of his car, he zoomed down to the next corner.

"When you get to the next corner, turn left and pull into the first driveway you see and turn out your lights. When Delbert goes past he'll probably go to the next corner, slow down to see if we turned, then shoot on down the street. When he gets halfway down the next street, back out and let's head back to Stover and finish the job we started and burn that damn bridge. By the time Delbert figures out that we ditched him we'll be on our way down the road on the way to the Pard with a bridge burning behind us."

Just as the boys figured, the deputy's car drove right past them and headed on down the street. When he got nearly two blocks away Slick backed his car up and headed back down the road to the next corner, with his lights out, and turned back to Aspen, then back down the street to Stover. When he reached the street he headed directly to the next streetlight and pulled over, and Jerry leaned out the window, pulling the trigger, and another light burst, fizzled, and bit the dust.

When the last light burst and went black, they drove across the Stover bridge. Bobby was standing right next to the guard railing when Slick slowed his car down, rolled down the window, and said, "Hey, Bobby, you need some help?"

"Nope. Heard some tires laying rubber a few minutes ago—that you?"

"Yeah. Nothing to worry about, though. It was duffuse Delbert. We lost him somewhere over there, three or four blocks from here. He didn't even see us even though we drove right past him." Slick was smiling as he leaned out the window. "He's such a klutz—don't worry about it. Just torch the damn bridge when we pull over and stop around that corner. When you see us stop, light that torch and heave it under the bridge and high-tail it over here so we can jinx it."

Slick pulled the car around the corner and stopped. Both boys leaned out their windows turning their heads back to see Walt light the torch and sling it at and under the bridge.

Just like the torch did when it hit under the Seven Falls bridge, the gasoline exploded when Walt threw the torch. The force of the explosion knocked Walt backward and he landed on his butt. As soon as he hit the ground he jumped back up to his feet and ran to the waiting car.

"JESUS! Did you see that fucker explode!"

When he reached the right back door of the car, he opened it and jumped in, slamming the door behind him. The other two boys were still hanging their heads out the windows looking back at the inferno behind them. All they could say was "WOW!"

"Come on, you guys!" said Walt. "Let's get the hell out of here before somebody shows up."

Just as Deputy Delbert turned the corner onto Stover about ten blocks from where he first saw the boys in their car, he looked straight down the road toward the bridge. The night sky was lit up and the tips of huge, glowing flames could be seen flickering and dancing in the sky. He slowed down at first, then slammed his right foot down on the gas pedal. When he dropped down the hill just above the Stover bridge, he switched his foot from the gas pedal to the brakes, coming to a screeching halt half a block away from the burning bridge. He had driven about halfway down the hill when he stopped, the tips of the flames from the bridge just about eye level to him. Reaching down to find his radio mike on the seat next to him, he slowly brought it up to his mouth. "Boss," he stammered into the radio, "you're not gonna believe this when I tell you what I'm looking at…"

Chapter *Twenty-Eight*

"Where in the hell do you suppose that crazy, chicken-shit Zero ran off to?" Jim said as he and Howie were driving down Cheyenne Boulevard on their way to help Bobby set the Will Rogers bridge on fire.

"I don't have a clue, but when he does show up we ought to pound the living pud right out of him. I sure as hell don't envy him when Slick finds out what he did—he'll beat him to an ever-lovin' pulp."

The two boys were about four blocks from the Will Rogers bridge when Howie saw someone running across the road in front of him about fifty yards ahead of the car.

"There's the little sucker right now! Let's just keep going even if he tries to flag us down."

"Howie, we'd better see if we can pick the slob up," Jim replied. "If he gets caught he'll sure as hell squeal on all of us. There he is, hiding behind that big pine tree over there." Jim was pointing past Howie at Zero's poor attempt to elude them.

Just as Howie started to slow the car down, he rolled down his window and shouted, "Hey, you little cock-sucker! Get your ass over here right now! I mean it, Zero! Get over here now and get in before somebody comes down the road! We see your ass, now come here!"

Zero came out from behind the big tree and sauntered across the street in a kind of jog. He looked up and down the street, then came over to the car with his head hanging low, not wanting to look the other two boys in the eye.

"What the fuck do you think you were doing? Get in the back seat right now and just sit there. We don't even want to hear a damn word out of you."

Zero opened the door and slid into the back of the car. "Hey, guys, I'm really—"

Jim turned around and reached over the back of the front seat to grab Zero by his lapel while holding his other hand in a tight fist just inches away from Zero's face. "One more fucking peep out of you and I'm gonna smash you right in the mouth. Now just sit there and shut up, you lousy, yellow bastard." Jim's jaws were clenched tightly together, and the words just kind of hissed through his teeth, his lips tight and barely moving. He curled his hand that was on Zero's lapel, almost lifting the boy out of his seat. His fist opened and he slapped Zero hard across the face. Zero's head snapped to the left, and Jim threw him back against the back seat. Tears came to Zero's eyes, and he started sobbing while pushing himself firmly against the back of the seat and looking down at the floorboard of the car. Jim was still leaning over the seat. "That's right!" he snarled. "You big chicken-shit baby. Just sit back there and ball your eyes out like the little fairy you are. You just wait until the rest of the guys get their hands on you." Jim turned back around and settled into his seat, looking over to Howie. "He's gonna be one sorry, dead son-of-a-bitch."

For the next half-dozen or so blocks the three boys rode along in complete silence. Howie broke the silence just as they were coming up on the Will Rogers intersection. Howie looked in his rearview mirror right at Zero. "Now, you slimeball, listen up," he said. "When we get to the Rogers bridge all three of us are gonna get out and help Bobby." Zero made no reply

Just as they approached the bridge a car came down the road and across the bridge. Bobby wasn't anywhere in sight, and Howie just kept driving until he was on the other side of the bridge. The other car's lights turned bright as it came to a stop at Cheyenne Boulevard, then went dim again when they pulled out and around the corner heading west.

After the other car disappeared around the corner, Howie turned in the first driveway he came to, backed up, and headed back across the bridge. Just as Howie crossed the bridge Bobby's head popped up over the guardrail. When he saw that it was his buddies, he came out from under the bridge and ran over to the car as Howie pulled over to the curb.

"Man, am I glad to see you guys!" he said. "I thought for sure something'd happened when it got past 10:30 and you didn't show." He was standing next to the open window on Jim's side of the car. "How'd it go? Did you do it? Hey, what's up with Zero?"

Jim started to open his door, and Bobby stepped back and away as Jim stepped out of the car. Howie was getting out on the other side and looked through the back door's window at Zero. "Get out of there right now, dip-shit!"

As Zero slowly opened his door and started to slide out of the car, Howie leaned over and grabbed the boy by his shirt and roughly pulled him out and pushed him toward the back and around the rear of the car. Zero stumbled around the car and was soon standing right next to Jim and Bobby with Howie shoving him on the back from behind.

"This dumb-shit chickened out and ran just as we were heading across the Falls bridge with the power company truck right on our tail." Howie looked down at Zero, then at the other two boys while still grasping Zero's shirt. "Now this sorry son of a bitch is gonna have the honors of torching this bridge or I'm gonna pound his ass right into the ground here and now." Howie pulled Zero right up to his face. "Isn't that right, mother-fucker?"

Zero had both hands around Howie's arm that was holding on to his shirt. He didn't say anything, just shook his head in agreement. Then he said, "Yeah. Yeah. I'll do it. I'll do it. Now get your hands off me." But Howie kept his grip on the boy's shirt and slowly let him go with a rough push that sent Zero back against the side of the car.

Bobby looked over at Howie just as he released Zero and pushed him against the car. "You mean this little bastard chickened out and ran?" Then he stepped up and got right into Zero's face. "Why, you little no good, worthless SOB. You could've gotten Howie and Jim caught along with the rest of us!" Then he shoved Zero back against the car again. "Who the hell do you think you are?"

Howie reached over and pulled Bobby back away from Zero and said, "OK, you guys, we have to pull ourselves together and torch this bridge and get the hell out of here PDQ or we're all gonna get caught. Where's the torch?"

Bobby ran back over to the bridge and disappeared, then came back up a minute later with the torch in his hand. "Here it is, and it's all soaked with gas and ready to go." He handed it to Howie, who pushed it into Zero's chest.

"Here, dip-shit. Now hold it over here so I can light it. As soon as it starts burning, you run right over next to the bridge and throw it directly underneath."

As Jim listened to Howie's instructions to Zero, he started to say something. Howie held up his hand and looked at Jim, waving him back with his other hand. "But—" Howie held his left index finger up to his lips, indicating to Jim to be quiet.

Howie continued with his instructions. "After I touch my lighter to the torch, we'll stay right here and you go torch the bridge. If you chicken out, so help me God I'll run your ass over with the car. Now get going."

Zero slowly advanced on the bridge, holding the torch high in his hand and straight out in front of him.

"Jesus, Howie," Jim said, "he'll blow his ass up if he gets too close. We'd better tell him not to get too close. Remember how the Falls bridge exploded and knocked us on our face? Hell, it'll blow him to smithereens."

"Naw. He won't get hurt, but I bet it'll scare the livin' shit out of him." Howie had a big smile on his face and watched intently as Zero walked toward the bridge. When the boy was about thirty feet away, Howie hollered, "THROW IT UNDER THE BRIDGE NOW!"

Zero swung the torch behind him and heaved it under the bridge. Within a split second the bridge exploded in a huge, hot ball of flame. Zero never even had a chance to turn completely around before the force of the blast caught him and lifted him fifteen feet off the ground, almost straight up into the air and half the distance back to where the other three boys were standing. When he hit the ground, rather than springing to his feet he just started crawling in super fast motion as if he were in a swimming pool doing the frog stroke. He wasn't making much forward progress, but he sure was moving his arms and legs like he was traveling a mile a minute.

Because Jim and Howie had experienced the explosion at the Falls bridge, they didn't react much to the inferno in front of them now, except to shield their eyes from the brightness of the flames. Bobby, on the other hand, jumped straight up and behind his two friends with both of his arms high in the air. "Holy shit!" was all he could say.

"Yeah, ain't it somethin'? Look at that sucker burn," Jim said, watching the flames from the bridge reach a good hundred feet into the sky. The light from the fire lit up the surrounding area like broad daylight, and the boys could feel the intense heat from the flames on their hands and faces.

"Lookit Zero!"

All three boys looked down and over at Zero, who was still trying to swim his way back to the car on the gravel berm next to the road. He hadn't made ten feet when all three of the boys laughed in unison and rushed over to Zero, who was also screaming at the top of his lungs. When they reached him, they bent down and grabbed Zero by his arms and lifted him up to his feet and started pushing him forward ahead of them toward the car. They didn't have to push very long before Zero lit out on his own, running right past the car and down Will Rogers Road, directly toward Cheyenne Boulevard

"Hey, Zero! STOP!" Jim hollered and took off after Zero. The other two boys were right behind him. The three boys finally caught up to Zero just before he made the corner. Jim leaped forward off his feet, tackling Zero, and both boys hit the ground with a thud and rolled over. By the time they started to roll over, Howie was on top of Zero, grabbing him by his shirt and lifting him up to his feet. "What the fuck do you think you're doing?! We've got to get the hell out of here!" And he turned the boy around and shoved him back toward the car. "Now get your ass back to the car and get in!" Turning back to Bobby and Jim, who were just getting up off the ground, he swung his left arm in a forward circle shouting to the other boys to get going.

After opening the right rear door to the car, Howie shoved Zero into the back seat, slammed the door shut, and ran around to the driver's side and jumped inside. He hit the ignition switch, and the car was running before the other two boys were in the car. He slammed the gearshift into reverse and peeled out backward, cranking the steering wheel hard to the left, then shoving the gearshift into first. Foot flat to the floor on the accelerator, the car lurched forward with tires screaming and raced to the intersection. Howie shifted into third as they turned the corner, heading down Cheyenne Boulevard to the Eighth Street turnoff.

Zero was shaking all over and whimpering to himself in a low, moaning sound. Howie looked in the rearview mirror, and Jim turned and looked back over the seat while Bobby looked over at Zero and pushed himself against the opposite door. When they all focused on Zero, their looks were those of pure amazement. Zero looked up and blood was dribbling down both of his cheeks, and when he lifted his hands up, both palms we all bloody.

"Look what you did! I'm gonna bleed to death and die and it's all you guys' fault!" He lowered his head and started to cry again.

Howie turned on his dome light so the other two boys could get a better look at him.

"Awww, shut up, you big baby," Bobby said quietly. "All you've got are a few little scratches. Here let me help." Bobby leaned over and pulled Zero's shirt out of his pants and lifted the tails up to Zero's face and started rubbing the boy's face. Zero snapped back and away, but Bobby followed his movements and continued to rub his face with the cloth. "See, all you got was a few little scrapes. Now, take your shirt and clean yourself up. When we get to the Pard you can go into the john and wash yourself up. What are a few scratches anyway?"

Zero was still crying when he took his shirttails and started to rub his face. The other boys laughed as the taillights of their car turned off Cheyenne Boulevard onto Eighth Street. Behind them in the distance, the glow of two huge, separate fires could be seen lighting up the horizon to the west.

Chapter *Twenty-Nine*

Daddy Bruce was doing sixty miles an hour with his bubble light swirling on the top of his patrol car and his sirens blaring as he was moving in and out of the few cars that were on Penrose Boulevard heading to the main bridge that intersected Penrose and Highway 85. When he was a little over a mile away he could see all the way down the road to the bridge. He could see a pickup way ahead of him, and it was pulling up under one of the last of two lights still burning along the entire boulevard. Just as he saw the distant light flutter and go out, Deputy Delbert's voice came over the radio.

"They just torched the Stover Bridge, boss! Just before I was gonna cross it, the whole thing just blew up in a wall of flame!"

"I know, I know, you crazy bastard! The light guys just called and said the Seven Falls bridge is also burning, and I can see flames shooting up over at the Rogers bridge too. And I can see a pickup straight ahead of me here on Penrose, and they just shot out a light and it looks like they have one more to go—the whole damn place is either on fire or completely black. I can see them pulling away from the light, and they're really hauling ass down to the next one. They just turned out their lights, so it looks like they see me. Get your butt over here as fast as you can. Head over to the Alsace bridge and see if you can hit Cheyenne Boulevard to 85 and cut them off. Move it out now!"

"Roger, boss. I'm heading out right now. Ya think I should radio the fire department about these fires?"

There was a pause in Delbert's radio reception then a heavy wheeze before his boss's voice boomed over the speaker, "What the hell do you *think*, you dumbshit! Of course call the fire department! Now get your ass over to Alsace and come up behind these guys."

"Yes, sir. Right away."

"Bob and Chuck, you guys still around?" The sheriff released the thumb button on his microphone so any incoming messages could be heard.

"Yeah, Daddy, we're here. You gotta know that the Falls bridge is burning also. What do you want us to do?"

"Yes, I know, and they blew up the Rogers and Stover bridges too. Did you get a chance to see who torched the Falls bridge?"

"Couldn't see a thing with all the fire. All we saw was a car but couldn't tell what make it was, and they were too far away to see a license number or anything else. From what we could tell, it looked like two men but don't even know that for sure."

"Damn!" The sheriff paused. "Just in case Delbert screws up, why don't you guys call the fire department and tell them to get moving?"

"Sure would but we can't—don't have their frequency on our radio."

"Then just get your asses over to the firehouse as fast as you can and tell them what's going on. Over and out!"

"Copy. Over and out."

Just as the power company truck pulled around the corner next to the firehouse, the garage door was going up and one of two big red trucks started to pull away. Bob slammed on his brakes and slid over to the far curb just missing the fire truck. Before their truck came to a full stop, Chuck was out and running across the street. He burst into the front door of the firehouse, shouting for the men to get the other truck going as fast as they could.

"We're shorthanded and don't have enough guys to work the other truck." A big man was standing in front of Chuck. Bob came through the door, slamming it all the way around until it hit hard on the wall behind it.

"What do you *mean* there aren't enough men for the other truck? There's a bunch of maniacs out there burning all of the fuckin' bridges! Call somebody! Do something!"

Both men were standing side by side looking straight at the lone fireman, his shoulders shrugging up and down and head shaking back and forth with a lost expression on his face.

Bob looked at Chuck, then back at the fireman, "We can drive the damn thing if you'll show us what to do and handle the hoses. Can you do it?"

"My name's Harley," the fireman said. He stuck out his big hand and shook Bob's first, then moved his hand over to grasp Chuck's. "Goddamned right I can handle those hoses," he looked over both men quickly. "Let's go!"

Within minutes all three men slipped into firemen's suits, threw open the big garage door, and guided the second fire truck down the road. "The first truck headed over to the Falls bridge," Harley said. "Let's head over to Stover."

With sirens crashing the quiet night air, the big red truck turned the corner and moved out of sight down the dark street toward the second big blaze, lighting up the night sky to the north.

Jeannie and Jennifer had been sitting in Old Ironsides for about thirty minutes when they saw the first yellow-orange glow reaching high into the sky a long way to the west of where they were parked.

"Jeez, Jen, you see that? Don't suppose that's the flame from the Seven Falls bridge, do ya?"

Both girls looked at each other, then back at the bright glow in the sky. Just as the glow grew brighter in the sky, another glow started to light up the sky even closer to them.

"Shit, Jeannie, there goes Stover! Those guys are actually doing it!"

Just as Jeannie and Jen were watching the second glow to the west intensify, a set of car lights came screaming down the Alsace hill and across the bridge right in front of them. It was Gill and Rick. Gill put on his bakes and skidded to a stop right next to the girls' car. Rick had his window rolled down. "You chicks get the hell out of here!" he said. "We'll handle this. Did you guys pour the gas on the bridge yet? Where's the torch?"

Jeannie was sitting shotgun and she clambered out of the car and quickly hopped over to Rick, who was already starting to get out of his car.

"We did the best we could," she said, "and we put some on the torch too." She went back to her car and reached over the back of the front seat and grabbed the torch, bringing it out and handing it to Rick. "Jeez, that stuff really stinks. Here, you take it." Jeannie turned and looked back into her car. Talking to Rick, she looked at Jen, who was sitting behind the steering wheel but bending down along the front seat so she could see Rick. "But we'd like to stick around 'til you light the bridge on fire." Looking westward, she pointed at the glows in the horizon. "Did you guys see those lights in the sky over there?"

Rick and Gill both turned and looked west.

"Damn! They did it!" Rick said out loud and to nobody in particular. "Let's set this damn bridge on fire and get the hell out of here!"

Rick took the torch from Jeannie. "You chicks stay here while Gill and I go over and throw this thing under the bridge. Where did you spread the gas?"

"Mostly along the far side. Didn't have enough to soak both sides. You guys be super careful, OK?" Jeannie said, pointing to the far side and indicating the underside of the bridge.

Rick and Gill started to walk toward the bridge. Rick moved the torch over and in front of Gill, who had already lit a match and was holding it out in front of him. When the flame hit the cloth covering the end of the sawed-off broomstick it burst into flame. The quickness of the torch bursting into flame startled the boys and they both took a quick stumbling step backward. "Whoa!" Rick said. "That sucker really caught on fast. Maybe we better not get much closer, Gill. Throw it from here."

Both boys turned and looked back at the girls, who were sitting in Ironsides. They shrugged their shoulders in unison and turned back toward the bridge. Rick put the torch down beside him, then lifted it quickly over his head as fast as he could and released it when it reached the top of the arch. The torch sailed down and under the bridge, and before it hit the ground the gasoline-laden bridge supports burst into flame. The boys' faces lit up brightly from the instant inferno in front of them. They both jumped a good two feet straight up into the air, and when they hit the ground they turned and ran as fast as they could back to the car. They could see the girls' faces shining like candles behind the windshield of the car where they were sitting. Both Jen's and Jeannie's eyebrows were raised high and their mouths were wide open, but the boys couldn't hear anything the girls were obviously saying.

The boys could feel the intense heat of the fire behind them as they ran toward the car. Gill was waving his right hand at the girls, shouting for them to get going. Gill had left his car running so when they split to go around each side of the door, both boys opened their doors and jumped into the car. Before Rick even had his door shut, Gill had the car in gear and was peeling out, heading down Alsace to the intersection of Cheyenne Boulevard.

Jeannie's hand was shaking when she tried to put Ironsides in gear. She was trying to force the car's gears, then remembered to push on the clutch and the gearshift slid into place. When she popped the clutch, the car died. Fumbling around in a panic she grabbed the keys in the ignition, turned it, and the engine jumped to life once again. She slammed the clutch to the floor, slipped the gearshift down, eased up on the clutch, and the car moved away from the curb. All of this seemed like it took hours, but it actually only took a few seconds before they were turned around and following Gill's car up to Cheyenne Boulevard. Jennifer was screaming at her friend to get going, but Jeannie didn't even seem to hear her. By the time they turned onto Cheyenne and were moving right behind the two boys ahead of them, both girls went completely silent until Jennifer said, "My God!" and glanced over at Jeannie who was staring her right back in the eye, "Did you see that son of a bitch explode?" As they followed Gill down the road both girls started to laugh hysterically.

Chapter *Thirty*

Daddy Bruce was hitting seventy miles an hour right toward the truck that was pulling under the last streetlight on his side of the Penrose bridge. He had his radio mike up close to his mouth and was screaming into it, "Delbert! Delbert! Come in. Delbert, are you there?"

"10-4, chief. I copy you loud and clear."

"Get your butt down to highway 85 NOW! I've got those little bastards in my sights. Damn, they just shot out the last light and are pulling away and heading over the bridge. Where are you? Damn it, Delbert, where the hell are you right now?!"

"I'm just turning down Alsace now and will be heading down the hill in just a sec."

"Well, get moving! If you don't move it, they're gonna hit the highway and be gone. Wait a minute—they just pulled over to the side of the road on the other side of the—"

"Holy shit! Boss, the Alsace bridge just exploded in front of me! Jeeze!"

Deputy Delbert slammed on his brakes and cranked his steering wheel hard to the left, forcing his patrol car into a sideways slide down the steep hill. Sliding sideways and slowly turning backward, the car skidded right toward the burning bridge. Delbert had his mouth wide open, but no sounds were coming out. All he could do was grip the steering wheel as hard as he could while holding the brake pedal to the floor. His eyes were scrunched tightly shut as he crouched forward, expecting to feel the impact of his car as it careened into the burning inferno of flame. Even though the patrol car came to a safe halt a good hundred yards away, the deputy was still crunched over the steering wheel with both hands grasping the wheel and his foot firmly on the brake pedal. In a few moments he realized that the car wasn't moving anymore. With his voiceless mouth still wide open, he slowly opened his eyes and turned his head to look into the flames coming from the bridge and shooting high into the night sky. Sweat was pouring from his forehead and his armpits were soaking wet. When the screaming voice of Daddy Bruce came through his radio speaker, it startled Delbert out of his silent, stationary panic, and a slow high-pitched screech shattered the quiet of the inside of the patrol car. The shriek made Delbert jump, even though it came from his own mouth. Moving at the speed of an old-time movie, he swirled in his seat and grabbed the mike of his radio.

"B-b-boss, I'm here, b-but I'm never gonna make it to the h-high-way."

"What do mean, you idiot? Get your butt moving and get over there right now!"

"I c-can't, boss. The Alsace bridge just exploded into flame, and I almost ended up right in the middle of it, and—"

"Exploded? Alsace? You mean they blew that son of a bitch too?"

"Yes, sir. It's burning pretty damn good."

There was a pause before the sheriff pushed the broadcast button on his mike again. "Then get your behind over here right away. I've got 'em trapped and will have their butts in custody in just a few minutes. Don't know what they're up to, but they just walked away from their truck back toward the bridge. Delbert, get over here PDQ. I could need a little help."

"Boss, did you say they were walking back toward the bridge?"

"Yes, Delbert. They're walking to the bridge. The little bastards think they have it made, but I'm gonna be on top of them before they know it." Delbert could hear his boss's hideous chuckle. "They were carrying something with them. Guess they're gonna have a picnic."

"Hey, boss, you don't suppose they're gonna—"

"Shut up, Delbert. Just get moving."

"Yes, sir, but maybe they're—"

"Delbert, I don't want to hear anything else from you. Get over here, NOW!"

"But, boss—"

"Delbert, Delbert…" There was a short moment of silence, then, "Ohhhhhhhhhh! Ieeeeeeee!"

Delbert just sat in his seat staring at the speaker under his dashboard, listening to the strange sounds coming from it. The high-pitched vocal sounds coming from his boss were followed by the loud screeching of tires locked in place on pavement. And then no more vocal sounds came through the speaker—only the sound of rubber leaving its mark on the road. Delbert always wondered how long it would take a car to come to a complete stop when it was moving at a high speed; from the length of time the screeching sound came from the speaker, it took a lot longer than he expected. Just as the sound of tires gripping asphalt started to fade away, his boss's voice burst from the speaker once again. "Oh nooooooooo!" This was followed by the loud crash of bending metal, broken glass, then complete silence.

"Boss? Boss, you all right? Mr. Bruce, are you there?"

Delbert let his mike fall to his pants. Just before he started to put his car in gear, a soft, muttered sound came from his radio speaker.

"Delbert, you there? Come in, Delbert, come in."

The deputy picked up his mike and nervously pressed the transmit button. "Boss, is that you?"

"Now, who in the hell do you suppose it would be?"

"Well—"

"Don't say a word, Delbert. Yes, this is the sheriff speaking. You need to come over here right now. I've had a slight accident. My car is wrapped around the last light pole on the east end of Penrose Boulevard, and I can't get out. Would you please get your little body over here RIGHT NOW? Oh, and Delbert, you won't have a hard time finding me because just a few hundred feet in front of me there's a huge fire that lights up the entire area. From where I'm sitting I can see through the flames where those two guys are standing next to their pickup as we're all three watching the Penrose bridge burn from both sides. Whoever those two guys are, they're standing over there waving at me."

"Boss, you all right?"

The sheriff was talking in a quiet voice now.

"Yes, Delbert, I'm just fine. Now would you please get over here so I can get out of this mess?"

"Right away, sir. I'm coming right now. You just sit tight and I'll be there in a flash."

With the last bridge burning brightly in the late night sky, Bill and I stood on the east side of the blazing bridge waving at the patrol car that was sitting completely still next to the last streetlight that had been shining brightly just moments before. We turned to each other and shook hands. With one final glance over our shoulders we gazed over the flames of the Penrose bridge to the west, where there were four more sets of bright balls of glowing light illuminating the western sky.

Chapter *Thirty-One*

A thick cloud of steam was rising from under the hood of Daddy Bruce's car. The sheriff was leaning back against his seat, squinting his eyes to look through the rising steam and through the bright flames from the bridge. Both boys were waving at him, then turned and climbed into their truck. As they drove away, they extended an arm out each side of the truck, giving the sheriff a final single-finger salute. The flames from the bridge engulfed their image and they were gone from sight.

When Deputy Delbert pulled up behind the sheriff's car, all he could see were two booted feet having a tantrum on the driver's-side window. Running up to the door, the deputy leaned in and peered into the window.

"Mr. Bruce! Mr. Bruce, you all right?"

At first the sheriff didn't acknowledge his deputy. He just lay back on the front seat and continued to try to break the window with his feet. The deputy stepped back, waving both hands, palms out in front of him. "Sheriff, don't worry! I'll get you out of there."

Daddy Bruce quit kicking at the window and dropped his feet down to the seat. With his knees bent and both feet flat on the car seat, he spread his legs and looked up at Delbert. He had a tight smile of pure fury. "Get me out of this damn thing right now!" he hissed.

The deputy reached down to the door handle and frantically pushed the button that should have released the door lock and started jerking back with all the strength he could muster. The door didn't budge.

"Don't worry, boss—I'll figure something out!"

Looking through the door window and down at his boss lying on the seat, Delbert could see the sheriff's smile fade and turn to a straight, tight-lipped expression.

"Go get the crowbar out of your trunk and pry the damn door open!" the sheriff shouted.

Just as Delbert turned and started to trot to the back of his car, he saw the utility truck pull up behind his car.

Almost before the truck came to a complete stop, Bob and Chuck were out and running toward the deputy. Delbert stopped and waited for them to reach him. Within a few feet of where the deputy was standing, both men slowed to a walk and stopped.

"We overheard the sheriff's call for help and came as fast as we could. What the hell happened?" Chuck said. Neither man looked at the deputy but gazed past him at the flames from the Penrose bridge shooting into the night sky.

Without waiting for a response from the deputy, Bob turned and started to run back to the truck. "I'll get a pry-bar so we can get Bruce out of there just in case there might be a gas leak and the son of a bitch explodes."

Within seconds Bob returned with the pry-bar and walked right between the other two men, lifting the pry-bar toward the frame of the front door and the middle support post. Looking into the front seat, he gave the sheriff a quaint smile and motioned with his free hand. "Don't worry, Sheriff Bruce, we'll have you out of there in a jiffy."

The sheriff was sitting up now and was on the passenger side of the front seat.

Chuck came up behind Bob and motioned for the sheriff to lie back down, "Sheriff, just lie back down and put both of your feet against the door and push with all the strength you've got."

Bob positioned the flat end of the bar and worked it in between the space of the door and center post. Once it was wedged in tight, both men grabbed the end of the bar and put their combined weight against it. "PUSH!" The two husky men leaned into the bar and the sheriff pressed both feet against the inside panel of the door, braced his hands back behind his head flat against the panel of the passenger door, and pushed as hard as he could. The sheriff's face turned bright red as he held his breath, putting all of his inner strength into pushing against the door. On the outside Bob and Chuck grunted hard against the pry-bar. Squeaking, creaking noises came from the door as it fought against the pressures of the three men. Finally the two men let up on the bar and waved to the sheriff to ease off. "OK. Let's give it all we've got, on the count of three. I think we can get it this time." Chuck held his right hand up next to the window so the sheriff could see his fingers count off the chant of "One, two, three!"

The eerie sound of metal slipping against metal grew to a crescendo, and without any warning the door popped open, sending both men on the pry-bar slamming into the rear door of the car. Bob bounced off the car and fell backward onto the ground. Chuck staggered around trying to avoid stepping on his friend lying on the ground, and the sheriff's feet shot out of the door opening. As soon as he felt the freedom open up before him, he sat up and scrambled out of the car, reaching back behind him to grab his hat. Bob was up, and both men moved in to help the sheriff by grabbing both of his arms, pulling him away from the smashed patrol car. Delbert stood off to the side. "Boss, you all right?"

After they moved a short way from the car, the sheriff pulled his arms away from the grasp of the two utility men. All four men turned back toward the patrol car. The bubble light was still flashing and its spinning glow reflected ghostly intermittent streaks of light across their faces.

Coupled with the orange brightness of the burning bridge, it looked like a scene from a sci-fi movie. All four men just stood in the glow in a daze of disbelief, with the hissing of steam coming from the radiator of the patrol car and the loud crackling sound of the burning inferno of the Penrose bridge.

In a quiet voice the sheriff said, "Delbert, go radio for the fire department to get over here."

Before Delbert could respond to the sheriff's orders, Bob spoke up. "Won't do any good, sheriff," he said. "All the units have responded to the Will Rogers and Seven Falls bridges. They won't be able to get over here for quite a while."

"Damn! Has anybody called the Springs' department for help?"

"Chuck and I called them as soon as we saw the flames from the Stover bridge, but all they could send was one truck because of an apartment fire they were responding to on the east side of town."

The conversation remained subdued as the fire burned in front of them. They started to back away from the heat. When they reached the deputy's car, all four men leaned against its side. The bubble light on top of Delbert's car was flashing, sending pulsing streaks of reddish orange light across the backs of the men's heads.

Delbert turned to his three comrades and asked, "What in God's name happened tonight? Do any of you guys realize that there isn't one single way off of this hill? The entire community of Brookshire is completely blocked off!"

The other three men didn't turn to Delbert, but just kept staring toward the flames. "Yup," they said in unison.

"Who the hell would ever want to do something like this?" Bob asked.

"And why?" Bob shook his head in response.

The sheriff leaned up against the car and crossed his feet as he watched the bridge burn. "Whoever it was had one hell of a plan. It must've taken fifty men to pull this off. At least fifty.

"Well, men, we'd better get over to the bridges where the fire guys are and see if we can lend a hand. It won't be long before we start getting calls from the press, and reporters will start swarming all over the place asking questions we don't have answers to. I can almost see the headlines in tomorrow's paper."

The four men pushed off and away from the deputy's car. Each moved slowly with slumped shoulders in a look of defeat. Chuck and Bob walked to their truck and got in while Daddy Bruce moved around to the passenger side of Delbert's patrol car, opened the door, and sat down in the seat. Delbert was already behind the steering wheel.

"Turn off your bubble, Delbert. We don't need it now. Let's just head over to the Falls bridge and see how things are going over there."

As the two officers turned and headed west on Penrose, the glow of the Seven Falls bridge was just a low glimmer in the sky. There were three other bright lights to their right, and Delbert could still see the flames from the Penrose bridge filling his rearview mirror.

Chapter *Thirty-Two*

"Damn, Old Man Bruce really wiped out on that light pole," Bill said as he was turning his truck left off Highway 85 and onto Cheyenne Road. "It was like looking through the fires of Hell when we waved to him sitting there inside the cop car. Hope he didn't get hurt—sure don't need that kind of trouble."

"Yeah," I agreed. "It was scary when I saw him hit the pole, but it looked like he was doing fine the way he was moving around inside. Man, I'll bet he's madder than all get out.

"I wonder how the rest of the gang did? From the looks of the glows in the sky all the bridges are burning. Wow! Would you look at that!" I was leaning forward in the cab of the pickup looking over toward the four lights in the sky to the west. I looked over to Bill and with a big smile I shouted, "We did it!" Then, we gave each other a high five.

When we reached Eighth Street, we turned and headed over the hill to the Pard. When we turned into the Pard's parking lot, we saw the rest of the gang standing next to the trunk of Ironsides. Jennifer and Jeannie were the first to spot us driving into the lot and pushed their way past the other boys and ran out to meet us. The two girls split, each going to the respective sides of the truck. Even before Bill brought the truck to a complete stop, both girls were hanging on to the sides of the doors. Bill and I had rolled down our windows and both leaned out to give our girls a quick kiss as the rest of the gang whooped and cheered, fists swinging in the air. Bill and I stepped out of the truck and hugged the girls and strolled over to the rest of the guys. High fives and handshakes moved quickly around the group, but Bill was the first to say anything. Before he did, he put a single finger to his lips, letting out a quiet shushing sound. It took a little while for everyone to catch on, but eventually they quieted down enough so they could hear what Bill had to say.

"I know we did it, but we have to cool it down a bit. If you look around you can see that there are a lot of eyes and ears pointed our way from other cars in the lot."

Just about that time a couple of other kids who were in other cars walked over to the gang. "Hey," they said, "did you guys hear about what happened over at Brookshire?"

Slick looked at the boys. "Nope, we just got out of the movie. What's up?"

"Seems like someone or a group of someones torched every dang bridge leading up to Snob Hill!"

A couple of the gang members spoke in unison, "Every bridge? Naw, you gotta be jokin.'"

"Nope, just heard it on the radio. Look over the hill—you can see the glows in the sky over each one of the bridges." He paused for a minute then looked back at the gang. "Hey, you guys want to head over there to see what's going on?"

Bill spoke up first. "I don't know about the rest of you, but I've gotta get Jeannie back home before one, so we'd better get out of here."

I followed Bill's lead by saying, "Yeah, it'd be a kick to see what's going on, but Jen has to get home too." I held Jennifer closer and looked down at her. She was shaking her head in agreement.

"Aw, come on, you guys, don't be a bunch of frickin' party poopers! Let's go see what's happenin.'"

"Yeah, you guys," Zero chimed in, "let's go with them and see what happened to those poor—"

Before Zero could finish his sentence, Howie grabbed him by the shoulder and shoved him back behind Slick, who turned and gave Zero a look that said, *One more peep out of you, you little bastard, and I'll smear your stupid ass all over the parking lot!* Zero stood still and said nothing else.

"Come on, you guys. Old Zero there wants to go, don't you, Zero?"

Without even looking at Zero, Bill stepped forward and put his hand on the back of the boy, turning him back toward his car. "Naw, Zero's gonna stay with us. Besides, all of us better be heading home." The two boys headed back to their car, mumbling something about the gang being a bunch of chicken shits or something like that.

I left Jennifer standing next to Jeannie, and Bill and I moved into the center of the gang. "Hey, fellas," I said, "I know all of us are excited about what happened tonight, but if we stick around here we're gonna raise a lot of suspicion and probably say something to somebody that'll give us away. How 'bout I take Jennifer back home before she gets in trouble and let's all meet up at the cave in thirty minutes?" I looked back at Jennifer. "That cool with you, Jen?"

Reluctantly Jen shook her head in agreement. "I suppose. But, man, I sure would like to go up there to help you guys celebrate. This is a real bummer." Pouting, she headed around the rest of the boys and climbed into Ironsides.

Jeannie gave Bill a light squeeze around the waist and whispered to him, "Shit, I suppose you should take me home too. Damn it, why do you guys always seem to have all of the fun?"

As she turned to head back to the truck, Bill reached behind her and gave her a tiny tap on the butt. "Because us guys have to keep you little gals pure and sweet?" He had a sly smile on his face when he said it and it didn't leave his face even when Jeannie turned around like a bolt of lightning and slugged him in the stomach. By the sway of her hips, he could tell she wasn't too happy.

"Well, boys, we'll see you up at the cave in half an hour or so." With that he turned and jumped in his truck next to Jeannie, who slapped him hard on the leg as soon as he sat down. He just reached up behind her with his arm and brought her closer to his side, then tried to kiss her, but she turned away. "Doggone it, Bill, it just isn't fair!" Then she turned back to him, and he kissed her lips lightly before backing the truck out and heading onto Eighth Street. The rest of the gang jumped into their cars and followed right along.

I met Bill's truck at the mouth of the canyon and waved him over to the side of the road. Parked right next to me, Bill leaned over and rolled down his passenger-side window. "Well, how'd it go? Was Jennifer as pissed as Jeannie when you dropped her off?"

"Sure as hell was, but at least she didn't beat the ever-lovin' shit out of me like Jeannie did to you. Man, you have one wildcat for a woman— sure you're man enough to handle all of that?" I laughed out loud and waved Bill on ahead. "See you up there in a few minutes. I'll just follow you." Bill flipped me the bird, rolled up the window, and smiled back as he drove away.

The rest of the gang was already parked in front of the cave entrance, and only Slick was still standing outside. When Bill and I got out, Slick shook both arms in the air with clinched fists and walked briskly to meet us. With both fists now open, he gave us each high fives, then lowered his arms, one around the shoulders of each of us, and we all three walked into the cave.

Loud hooting and hollering could be heard inside the cave as we moved into the main room. The lanterns were lit, and all the guys were dancing around, hugging and giving each other a series of high fives. When Bill, Slick, and I moved into the room, the rest of the gang moved over to us in a single tiny mob.

"We did it! We fucking did it!" Walt shouted.

"Damn straight! We burned every damn bridge to the ground," Gill shouted right after Walt. "By God, Operation Blackout Brookshire is a success! Son of a bitch, we actually pulled it off!"

Howie moved ahead of the rest of the boys and shoved a long-neck bottle of Coors into Bill's, Slick's, and my outstretched hands. He turned back to the rest of the gang, held his beer high in the air, and shouted, "To the fucking success of Operation Blackout Brookshire!" And, the cave burst into another round of shouting and cheers of triumph. Foaming bottles were lifted up and tilted back and we all chugged our beers dry.

Howie was quick to start passing out more beer as the stories of each team's escapades were told. Pats on the back and handshakes honoring each team's success moved throughout the tiny group over and over again.

A couple of boys moved over and sat down on the sofa. Bobby shouted loud enough for everyone to hear, "OK, fellas, what the hell do we do for an encore?"

I moved to the back of the cave behind the folding card table and banged the butt of my beer bottle on the table. "Hey, hey, listen up, you guys!" I raised my voice again. "Come on, comrades, cool it and listen up for just a minute."

The boys slowly started to simmer down and the loud talk quieted down to a low murmur. "Aw, come on, Rock, let's celebrate! We don't need to get all serious right now. Give us a break."

"Yeah, come on, Rock," Jerry whined. "We just pulled off the hottest thing to happen around here since the gold-mine riots in the hills a hundred years ago, and we need to party!"

Roars of agreement lifted in the cave after Jerry and Bobby's little speeches. I stood my ground and banged on the card table again with the bottom of the bottle. This time Slick and Bill joined me in shouting down the rest of the gang members, telling them to cool it. Looks of disappointment slipped down over the faces of the other boys, but they eventually settled down with a few low grumblings of protest.

. "Men," I said, lowering my raised hands, "Operation Blackout Brookshire has been a success."

The room burst into shouts again, but I raised my hands, and Slick shouted for everyone to be quiet. The shouts subsided and I continued: "I don't know about the rest of you, but I didn't expect to see flames reaching two hundred feet into the air or for Daddy Bruce to nearly kill himself trying to run us down—"

"You mean old man Bruce tried to kill himself?" Bobby asked.

"Didn't you hear about Bruce wrapping his cop car around the pole just before he reached the Penrose bridge?" Jerry looked at Bobby with a curious look on his face. "Shit, I thought all of us knew about that. He was trying to get Rock and Bill before they torched the Penrose bridge, and he lost it and decorated the last light pole those guys shot out before burning the bridge. Lucky for us he wasn't hurt, though."

"Jesus," Bobby said, "I never thought of getting anybody killed over this thing."

"Well, we were lucky—and lucky that none of us were hurt, either," Jerry replied. "Who the hell expected gasoline to explode like that? Shit, we were damn near blown to hell and back when we torched the Falls bridge. Blew us right on our asses when the torch hit the gas, didn't it, Slick?"

Slick looked over at Jerry and nodded his head. "Damn right it did. Man, it was great!"

I hit the table with my bottle again, and the boys turned back in my direction. "Guys, we have to cool it for a while so we can see how this all falls out. I don't think Bruce, Delbert, or anybody else has a clue who we are, so let's just wait this thing out and see how everything shakes down tomorrow. In the mean time"—I was looking everybody in the eye—"not a word to anybody. Do you hear me? Not a word. We have to act just like everybody else and question everything that's said about tonight."

"Rock's right," Bill said. "If any one of us squeals one word about tonight, we're *all* going to the slammer. Not a word." And he held his hand up pointing a finger at everyone in the room until he came to Zero. "And you. If you so much as open your damn mouth and say one thing about what we did, I will personally see to it that you never see the light of another day. You hear me, Zero?"

Zero didn't say anything, just shook his head in agreement.

"OK, one more salute to the success of Operation Blackout Brookshire, and let's head it home." With that I held my beer bottle high and let out a loud "YAHOO!"

Just as we all started to head out of the cave, Slick waved for our attention. "Hey, fellas, before you head out, get your gas cans and put them into the back of my truck. I've got to get them back before my old man misses them."

"Yeah, and how about everybody meeting up here tomorrow afternoon around two o'clock?" I said.

Chapter *Thirty-Three*

"Hello, is Jennifer home? This is Ralph."

"Oh, hi, Ralph. Jennifer isn't in right now. I sent her to the store for some bread. She should be back any time so you might want to call back in a few minutes. And, my goodness, did you hear about the terrible thing that happened in Brookshire last night? It was just awful! Who in the world would do something as terrible as that? It just makes me sick, and it's really kind of scary, don't you think?"

"Yes, ma'am. I just heard a little bit about it but really don't know much."

"Ralph, according to the paper they think it was about fifty men who caused all of the trouble. They're calling it an organized gang and said it may be people who are opposed to what our government is doing over in Viet Nam. The reporter said they call themselves the Big Fifty. Isn't it just terrible, Ralph?"

I paused just a short moment after Mrs. Lucas's last statement. "The Big Fifty? That's what the *Free Press* actually called the people who did this? They really think it was fifty men who did this?"

"Yes, Ralph. Just a second and I'll get the paper and read some of it to you." I heard the soft thump of Mrs. Lucas putting the phone down on her kitchen counter and then the crinkling of paper in the background and pages being turned. I could hear the empty air sound of the phone being picked back up. "Ralph, you still there?"

"Yes, ma'am."

"Just listen to this. It was written by Jeff Jackson. He's one of the best reporters at the paper, and he knows what he's talking about."

"Yes, ma'am."

Mrs. Lucas started to read the article. At the other end of the phone I was sitting in a chair in the hallway between the kitchen and living room. I was slumped over with my elbows on my knees. I could feel beads of sweat running down the sides of my chest from my armpits and my palms were wet and clammy.

"Listen to this, Ralph: 'Last night the community of Brookshire was completely isolated from the greater Colorado Springs area by an organization thought to be made up of at least fifty members. Referred to as the Big Fifty, it is believed that this gang burned the bridges at the Seven Falls Road, Stover Road, Will Rogers Road, Alsace Way, and Penrose Avenue, and there doesn't seem to be any reason for such a devastating and destructible act. And why the Brookshire community was chosen is still the question that the Brookshire sheriff, Mr. Bruce, can't answer. His only comment was that he thought the Big Fifty was part of a national syndicated gang of mobsters who select certain communities of the country to attack, for no apparent reason.

"The sheriff completely totaled his patrol car while in pursuit of two of the gang members just before they set fire to the Penrose bridge.' And it keeps going on from there. Ralph, I sure hope they catch these Big Fifty troublemakers before they hurt anybody else. Makes me afraid to even go anywhere anymore." Mrs. Lucas paused for just a second. "Oh, Ralph, I think I hear Jennifer coming in from the store." She didn't hold the phone far enough away from her mouth when she hollered at her daughter telling her that I was on the phone. I quickly moved the phone away from my ear as Mrs. Lucas shouted at Jennifer. I switched the phone to my other hand and stuck my finger in my ear and wiggled it around in reaction to the sound blast from Jennifer's mother.

"She'll be here in just a minute, Ralph. Say, by the way, would you like to come over and join us for dinner tonight? We're having roast beef and would love to have you if you'd like to come."

"Thanks, Mrs. Lucas. I'll check with my mom and dad, and if it's OK with them I sure will. I'll let you know later, is that OK?"

"Sure, honey. Here's Jennifer. You have a good day."

I cringed everytime Mrs. Lucas called me honey, and this time was no different. I rolled my eyes and shook my head.

"Hi, Rock."

"Hi, babe. Man, did your mom show you this morning's paper?"

"Yes, I couldn't believe it." She was whispering into the mouthpiece. "The Big Fifty? I couldn't believe it, and man, was it hard just sitting there at the breakfast table while Dad read the paper to us. I was so nervous and couldn't look either him or Mom in the eye. They even asked me if there was anything wrong. I just said I was a little tired from staying up too late last night. They also asked me about the movies and I made up a bunch of stuff."

"You don't think they suspect anything do you, Jen?"

"Nope, but we better cool this conversation before they overhear me. Why don't you come over in a half-hour or so, so we can talk. I'm scared, Rock."

"Just stay cool, Jen. Everything's gonna be cool. Besides, I was calling to see if you could go up to the cave around one-thirty this afternoon. The gang's gonna meet up there. Man, I wish you could've been up there last night. It was wild."

"I don't know if they'll let me go because Mom is afraid of what happened last night and thinks we should all just stay close to home."

"Damn. But, hey, I think they might let you go out because your mom invited me over for dinner, and we can just say we're going over to the Pard for a Coke or somethin'. Why don't you go ask and I'll just wait here."

"OK. Hang on a minute. I'll be right back."

Before Jennifer put the phone down I quickly said, "Oops, oops, wait a minute! Just tell them that I checked with my folks and they said I could come over for dinner. Maybe that'll help."

"OK." Jennifer put the phone down and I could hear her footsteps on the kitchen linoleum. It wasn't but a minute or so before she was back.

"Rock, they said it was fine with them, but Mom wasn't too happy about it. Can you come a little bit earlier? I need to get out of here before I go nuts."

"I'll be there in a jiffy. Just hang in there, beautiful. See ya."

I put the phone down and leaned back in the chair pressing my head against the wall. I could feel the coolness of the plaster coming through the hair on the back of my head. In a very quiet, almost breathless whisper I spoke out loud and to myself, "The Big Fifty." In a moment I got up and headed to the front door. I was shaking my head slightly and had a confused smile on my face. Just as I was opening the front door, I leaned back and looked into the small den just off to the left of the doorway, where my mom was sitting in a chair reading a book. "Hey, Mom, do you suppose it would be all right if I had dinner over at the Lucases' house tonight? Jen's mother just invited me."

"Sure, sweetheart, but not too late. It's a school night, remember, and you've got to get your studies done and go to bed early." She was looking up from her book, smiling at me. "By the way, did you hear what happened up at Brookshire last night?"

"Yup. Mrs. Lucas just told me about it and read some stuff to me from today's paper. Wow, what a mess." I looked away from her, then turned back and said, "Thanks. See you in a couple of hours. I'm heading over to pick up Jen and we're going over to the Pard for a Coke and fries."

Just before I shut the door I heard my mother say, "OK, Ralph, but don't make it too long. Remember, you promised your father that you'd clean out the garage."

"You bet. I'll be home about four. See ya later." I shut the door behind me and ran over to my car, which was parked next to the curb in front of the house.

Chapter *Thirty-Four*

When I pulled into the Lucases' driveway, Jennifer was already coming out the front door. Mrs. Lucas was right behind her, following her over to the driveway. I got out of the car and walked around to meet them on the other side.

"Hi, ladies," I said, moving over to open the passenger door for Jen.

"Hi, Ralph," Mrs. Lucas said. "Now you two be real careful out there and don't go anywhere *near* Brookshire because I guess they have the whole place roped off."

I reached over and patted Mrs. Lucas on the arm. "You can count on that, Mrs. Lucas. We don't want to go anywhere near that place. We're just gonna head over to the Pard and will probably cruise around town for a while. I've got to get back around four so I can clean out the garage for Pop. I want to get done with that so I can hop over here for dinner." I took my hand off her arm and gave her a little wink, then turned to go around to the other side of the car. Jennifer had her window rolled down and her mother leaned into it with both of her hands on the sill.

"Don't worry, Mom," Jen assured her. "We're just gonna be gone for a couple of hours." She smiled up at her mother as she turned back toward the house. As we backed out of the driveway, Mrs. Lucas turned and waved. Jen and I both waved back at her as we drove away.

When we got a few houses away, she slid over next to me. It was a couple of blocks before either one of us said anything.

"Rock," Jen sniffled, holding onto my arm tightly but looking straight away. "I'm scared to death." She started crying.

Jen let my arm go as I lifted it up and put it around her shoulders. I pulled her nice and snug into my side. She leaned her head over onto my shoulder and started to sob. I could feel her trembling next to me and held her even tighter. When we came to a small park, I pulled Ironsides over to the curb, put it in park, and turned the key off. Shifting a little bit, I reached around her with my other arm and just held her as she cried in my arms. I could feel the dampness from her tears soaking through my shirt. I just held her as she cried and it was a couple of minutes before she pushed lightly against my body. I released my arms from around her as she sat up, looking me right in the eye. Her face was flushed, and tears were still running down her cheeks.

"Come on, babe," I said, "it'll be just fine. Just wait and see. Nobody has a clue who it was and everything will be OK." I leaned over and gave her a light kiss on the lips. When my lips touched hers, she pushed hers into mine with a sense of urgency. I put my arms around her again and kissed her hard. The kiss lasted a long time as we embraced each other. While we were kissing I caressed the back of her head, softly moving my hand over her hair. When we broke our kiss, she just snuggled her chin right onto my shoulder. I continued to hold her tight. "It'll be fine, just fine," I said in a whisper. "You'll see, it'll be just fine."

After a while I slowly pushed her away and leaned down to give her another soft kiss.

"I've got an idea," I said. "Let's just head over to the Pard and get a cherry Coke and some fries before we go up to the cave. How's that sound?"

Sniffling a bit and trying to regain her composure, Jen shook her head in agreement. I started the car and pulled away from the curb.

There were just a few other cars parked in the Pard's lot when we turned off Eighth Street into the ordering lane. Only one car was ahead of us as we pulled up to the next ordering speaker. Mrs. Harding's voice crackled through the speaker, "Welcome to Howdy Pard. Can I help you?"

"We'll take two medium cherry Cokes and a large order of fries."

"Is that you, Ralph?"

"Sure is, Mrs. Harding. How are you this afternoon?"

"Just fine. Have you got the sweet Miss Lucas with you?"

"Yes, ma'am, I'm here," Jen answered.

"Hi, sweetie. Say, did you folks hear about what happened up Brookshire way? It's just shameful! What do you suppose those nasty people were thinking? Someone told me that they figured there were at least fifty of 'em."

"Yes, ma'am, we heard about it. Don't really know what happened, though," I said back into the speaker. I reached down and held Jen's hand in her lap. I could feel that she was still trembling, and when Mrs. Harding asked the question Jen squeezed my hand hard.

"Well, kids, it was terrible. Now, you just be careful out there, you hear?" There was a slight pause. "You can move forward and I'll have your order out in a jiffy. Thanks, now."

"OK, Mrs. Harding. Thank you." I pulled up to the order window.

When Mrs. Harding opened the sliding window and leaned out with our order, she just shook her head, looking at us in the car. "Just some bad people out there, I guess."

I shook my head in agreement and handed her back the correct change. After giving the drinks and sack of fries to Jen, I pulled forward and moved across the parking lot to park by one of the lights. Mrs. Harding slid the glass window back into place a waved good-bye through the window as we drove away.

Jen took a sip of her drink and placed it on the dashboard in front of her. She broke open one of the small packets of salt and shook it out over the hot fries. Then she took two of the tiny cups of catsup and poured them over the fries. The smell of light grease filled the cab of the car as she lifted up the smothered fries, offering some to me. I grabbed a couple and stuck them in my mouth, followed by a quick drink of Coke. By the way I was chewing Jen could tell the fries were still very hot. When I looked over at her, she had a slight smile on her face.

"Everything's gonna be all right, isn't it?" she said looking at me. "Nobody knows who burned the bridges, do they?"

"No, honey, I don't think anyone has a clue. I can hardly wait to get up to the cave to see what the other guys have to say. The only one I'm worried about is Zero—if he stays cool everything will be fine."

"Boy, are you right about that lard-head. He could screw it up for all of us. I'm OK now. Let's head up there so we have some time before we have to get back."

I leaned over and gave Jen another peck on the lips and backed Ironsides out and started heading up to the cave.

As we turned and headed toward the mouth of the canyon, we could see the flashing lights of police cars down the streets to the south at almost every intersection we came to. When we reached the bottom of the canyon the entire road heading into South Cheyenne Canyon was roped off. Nobody even noticed us as we turned and headed up the north road.

When we turned onto the road leading to Hucky Cove, we could see that everybody was already there. Nobody was out in front of the cave's entrance, so we parked the car and headed right into the cave.

"It's about time you two showed up," Bill said. "We were wondering what happened to you or if you were even gonna make it. Thought something was up." Bill and Jeannie were standing to the left of the main group and were the first to notice us come into the room. "How 'bout a beer, you guys?"

I raised my hand with the Coke in it and gave a negative wave to Bill. Jennifer did the same as we moved into the small crowd in the center of the room.

"Well, what's up? Everything cool with everybody?" I looked around the room. I noticed that everybody was there except one guy. "Where's Zero?"

"No sweat. He just had to stay home and help his old man with something or other. He's cool," Gill said, raising his beer high in the air as a toast.

Walt moved forward. "Guess there isn't a Pikes Peak Gang anymore."

"What do you mean, no more Pikes Peak Gang? What happened?" I had a look of confusion on my face.

Almost in unison everybody else in the cave raised their arms with fists clamped shut and shouted, "We're the Big Fifty!"

Almost instantly Jen and I raised our hands high in the air and shouted, "We're the Big Fifty!" Our words sounded almost like an echo coming an instant after the rest of the gang's chant.

After a few minutes of robust shouting of the new name and everybody slapping each other on the back, the kids started to calm down a bit and the murmur of excited but quieter conversation started to fill the cavern.

"What do you think we should do now, Rock?" someone asked. Everyone turned to me, and I moved over to the table. Jen didn't move forward with me, moving instead over next to Jeannie, who was standing next to Bill with her arm around his waist.

Just as I was raising my hand to quiet the crowd, Bill looked over at Slick and both boys gestured for me to join them outside the cave. I moved out and around the table walking toward my two buddies, who were already moving out of the cave. "Hold on a minute, guys," I said to the rest of the group. "Looks like Bill and Slick want to talk to me about something. We'll be back in a shake." The three of us left the gang and disappeared, stopping when they reached the outside of the cave.

"What's up, fellas?" I said as I turned to face Bill and Slick.

Slick was the first one to speak. "Rock. Bill and I have been kind of talking about all of this and—" Bill looked at Slick and interrupted him.

"Yeah, we just don't think we should take this gang thing any further. We were lucky once, and if we keep this thing going, one of us is gonna screw up and all of us will be in big trouble."

"Bill's right," Slick continued. "I think we need to break this thing up before it gets out of hand. Besides, we did all of this because of the fight at the hockey game when they said we couldn't play there anymore. I don't think this is gonna help us get our team back on the ice anyway."

Both boys paused and waited for my response.

I looked at both of my friends and walked around in a short circle while looking down at the ground. After a minute or so I turned back to them. "Tell you what. I agree with you, but before we make our final decision, let's wait until tomorrow and see what happens at the school assembly. Depending on how that goes, we can make up our minds about whether we keep the gang together or shut it down. How's that sound to you guys?"

Bill and Slick looked at each other, then back at me. Slick nodded his head in agreement and said, "That sounds like a plan to me. What about you, Bill?"

"Sure. Hell, can't hurt to wait to see what happens."

The three of us shook hands and went back into the cave. None of the other members even seemed to notice we had returned and the conversation was getting louder. Jen and Jeannie were sitting on the couch next to the wall of the cave. All three of us moved up to the back side of the little table. Slick half shouted and banged his fist on the table to get everybody's attention. He had to shout a couple more times before everyone settled down and turned to listen to what their leaders had to say. Bill looked over at me and Slick, giving a nonverbal gesture that he would speak first. He casually looked each one of his friends and fellow members of the Big Fifty before he spoke.

"Rock, Slick, and I kind of got together to decide what we should do from here on out." He looked over at Slick and me, and we shook our heads in agreement. "To be honest with you, Slick and I told Rock that we thought we should break the gang up right now." There was a look of confusion on the faces of the rest of the members, and within seconds they all started to talk at once.

"What do you mean?"

"What are you guys talking about?"

"Shit, we can't quit now!"

The three of us raised our hands, gesturing for the rest of the boys to simmer down. Slick and I both shouted for everyone to calm down and let Bill finish speaking. It took a while, but eventually everyone quit shouting and Bill started to speak again.

"Damn it, now, you guys just take it easy and hear me out before you get all bent out of shape." He paused a minute to let that set in. "All of us know how successful Operation Blackout Brookshire was and we just thought we shouldn't press our luck." A low growl of discontent started up again when Bill raised both of his hands in the air, "Now, now, just wait a minute, fellas, before you start getting in a twist again." Everybody quieted down again but were a bit restless; shifting feet could be heard as the huddle of boys swayed back and forth on the rock floor of the cave. Jen and Jeannie just sat quietly on the couch. Bill went on: "As I said, Slick and I were ready to dismantle the gang right now, but Rock convinced us to wait until we see what happens at the school assembly tomorrow morning. So, we decided to wait until then before we make our decision."

I interrupted Bill. "Yeah, as you all remember, we started this gang because of what happened that night at the hockey game. Now, we'll just wait and see how it goes tomorrow at school. I don't think we accomplished a thing because everybody thinks that some other gang burned the bridges. At any rate, we'll just have to wait until tomorrow."

"Yup," Slick was about to take his turn talking to the gang. "What we'll do is see what Fudd has to say about all of this. After school we'll all meet out in the parking lot and see where we go from there."

"What do you think old man Fudd will say to us?" Walt said.

I answered him, shaking my head back and forth, "Don't have a clue, Walt. We'll just have to wait and see."

Bill nodded his head, then said, "Now, all of us have to remember to act as though nothing happened and that we're just as confused as everyone else." Bill looked over at Walt and Gill, pointing his finger at both of the boys. "You two guys. It's your responsibility to make sure that Zero doesn't say a word or screw up in any way. We're gonna hold both of you responsible for everything he does or says."

The room became almost completely quiet, then Gill said, "It's OK with me if it's OK with the rest of the guys." Everybody just kind of glanced around, looking at everybody else. Pretty soon, most of the boys agreed that waiting until the school assembly to decide the fate of the gang was fine with them.

"OK, then, let's break it up and see what happens tomorrow. Then all of us will meet after school down by the parking lot," I said, looking at Bill and Slick. "Let's break it up for today."

The gang slowly turned and started to exit the cave. The two girls moved against the flow to join their boyfriends. Bill and I each put our arms around our girls as we moved to leave the cave.

Chapter *Thirty-Five*

The next morning, about ten minutes after the tardy bell rang and the homeroom teachers had taken attendance, the buzzer of the intercom system coming on filled the classrooms. Moments later, Mr. Fluorite's voice crackled through the speakers: "Good morning, everyone. Would all students and faculty please report immediately to the gymnasium for a school assembly. Teachers, send your students to the gym now. Thank you."

As the students streamed out of their classrooms, the halls filled with the loud clatter of shoes on tile floors and the loud buzz of students talking as they passed through the doors to the gymnasium. Jennifer's room was closer to the gym than mine, so she backed out of the flow of the crowd and leaned up against the lockers to wait for me. When she saw me, she moved into the crowd and reached down for my hand. She looked up at me and asked, "Well, did Mrs. Fowler say anything about what Fudd's gonna say?"

"Nope. She just took roll and waited until the announcement came and then asked us to hand in our homework. How about Bamford? He say anything?"

"Huh-uh, not a word. I was kind of worried that he might ask me if you and I saw anything unusual over by the bridge when he stopped to talk to us when we were putting the cans out."

"Shhh! Man, girl, don't talk so loud and don't ever mention that again!" I said, looking Jen sternly in the face. Her eyes kind of got big and she said, "OK, already. I'm sorry."

As we funneled into the gym and moved up the bleachers to take a seat, Jen spotted Jeannie and Bill and motioned for them to come up and join us. She had made it a point to save some room for them to sit. Working their way up through the crowd Jeannie sat down next to Jen and Bill, next to his girl. Bill looked across, in front of the two girls and wrinkled his forehead in my direction in a questioning gesture. I just shrugged my shoulders and turned to look down to the podium in the center of the basketball court, where Mr. Flourite was standing. Almost simultaneously the principal's voice boomed over the speakers overhead: "May I please have your attention? Your attention, please! Come on now, let's quiet down so we can move along here. Thank you!"

It took a couple of minutes for the students to quiet down. Just a few voices could still be heard in the crowd when the principal began to speak again into the microphone.

"In just a few minutes, Sheriff Bruce from Brookshire will be here to address the student body. In the meantime, I would like to say a few words about what happened over this past weekend.

"As all of you know by now, there was some very serious vandalism that took place in the Brookshire area. All of the bridges were completely burned to the ground on every major road leading up to Brookshire as well as each and every streetlight shot out."

There was a light breakout of laughter throughout the students.

"Now, some of you seem to think this is pretty funny," Mr. Flourite continued. "All I can say is that those of you who think that have a pretty sick sense of humor." He paused and let his words take the effect he was hoping for, and the laughter subsided. "Originally it was reported by the newspaper in the Springs that this terrible act was done by a gang of at least fifty people. As Sheriff Bruce will tell you in a few minutes, the authorities now have a different perspective on exactly what happened."

Just about then, one of the double doors at the far end of the gym opened and the sheriff came strolling in, his heavy leather boots slapping on the hardwood floor. As he approached the speaker's podium, he removed his cowboy hat. At least two large bandages could be seen, one on the left side of his forehead and one just below his left ear. A low moaning sound came from the student body.

"Here is Sheriff Bruce now." Flourite looked down and gestured for the sheriff to join him on the podium, "Now, if all of you would please give Sheriff Bruce your undivided attention." With that, Mr. Flourite moved to the side of the microphone with his hand extended to shake the sheriff's hand. Bruce moved in front of the microphone as the principal stepped down from the podium and a few steps behind where the sheriff was standing.

I leaned forward and across the laps of the two girls between me and Bill. Whispering, I said, "What the hell do you think is going on?"

Bill just shook his head, but before he sat back up, Jen whispered into my ear, "Rock, I'm scared. You don't suppose he knows what happened." She was about in tears again and her hand squeezed mine tightly. I moved my mouth to her ear and whispered, "Don't worry, honey. If they knew anything they would have called us into the office rather than hold this meeting. Let's just wait and see what he has to say."

"Good morning, everyone." Bruce's voice boomed over the speakers, and he backed a bit further away from the mike. "As Principal Flourite has probably already told you, there was some serious vandalism that took place this past weekend. And the reason that I have been invited to speak to all of you today is to let you in on some of the information we have found out since the incident took place.

"At first we originally thought the criminals who committed these acts of violence were from out of the area and that there were at least fifty individuals involved. Now, however, we happen to believe that the people responsible for these outrageous acts could possibly be a large group of teenagers."

With that statement, the bleachers burst into loud, jumbled conversation. Principal Flourite moved up to the microphone immediately. "OK, now, let's have a little quiet here and let the sheriff continue. Quiet! Everyone, be quiet and let the sheriff speak."

The students quieted down once again.

"First off," Bruce continued, "let me explain that we do not—and I repeat, *do not*—know who any of these kids are, but we do believe that it is a group of teenagers who have formed a gang. Right now, we don't have any clues, nor are we pointing any fingers at any particular group or at any specific school in the area.

"What I am here for today is to ask each and every one of you to keep your eyes and ears open and, if you know of or hear anything that will help us bring these criminals to justice, to come forward immediately with any information you might have. Anything you might know will be held in complete confidence."

A quiet buzz was spreading through the group of students in the bleachers, but it wasn't loud enough to keep the sheriff from continuing to speak.

"One more thing. Before I say this, I want to make certain that you know that I am not accusing anyone or any specific group of students of anything. But all of us know that there are certain factions of people who were very upset when students who did not live in the Brookshire community were not allowed up there after the incident that took place after the hockey game a few weeks ago." The sheriff paused a moment to let his words to sink in. "Therefore, we want all of you to know that we're going to extend that rule until this problem is solved. Unless your family lives in the Brookshire community, you will not be allowed up there after eight o'clock every evening."

"That's bullshit!" The two words rang out across the gymnasium, but before anyone could actually see who said it, the rest of the students started to shout their concern over what was just said., Bill and I, however, knew immediately whose voice it was and looked up behind where we were sitting and spotted Gill with his hand over the mouth of Zero, who was sitting between him and Walt. "Jesus Christ" was all that I could say as I turned around and looked down at the sheriff again. I never even looked over at Jen or Bill. Both Sheriff Bruce and Principal Flourite were on the podium with their hands raised and asking for silence from the crowd. After the noise subsided again, the sheriff went on: "Like I said before, we aren't pointing any fingers at anyone. All we want is to ask for your cooperation while the investigation goes on and until we apprehend the people who are responsible for this action.

"We still believe that it has to be a large group of teenagers to have pulled this off, and they have taken on the name of the Big Fifty. If any of you knows anything about what happened over the weekend, I would appreciate it very much if you would contact my office so we can talk to you about it."

With that final statement, the sheriff thanked everybody and stepped down from the podium. Principal Flourite stepped back up to the microphone and dismissed the students, instructing us to go back to our classes. As the students siphoned through the gym doors, each member of the Big Fifty nudged one another and passed along a single sentence: "Don't forget the meeting in the parking lot after school."

When the final bell rang, dismissing school for the day, a small group of teenagers slowly worked their way down the paved hill to the parking lot down below the football field and huddled around an old Pontiac. From a distance, a shout of "The Big Fifty!" could be heard as they held their arms high in the air with their fists clenched tight and waving in the air.

About the Author

Jay S. Warburton was born in 1944 in Devil's Lake, North Dakota. From the age of 12 he grew up in Colorado, where he resides today. With the exception of 6 years as an intermediate and secondary teacher, he has made his living as a freelance photojournalist and video/movie producer specializing in outdoor themes. He has published hundreds of feature articles in fifty-two national and regional publications. As CEO and president of his own production company he has produced over 40 full-length videos under the title *The Sportsman's Video Library Series* with distribution worldwide. This is his first novel.